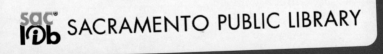

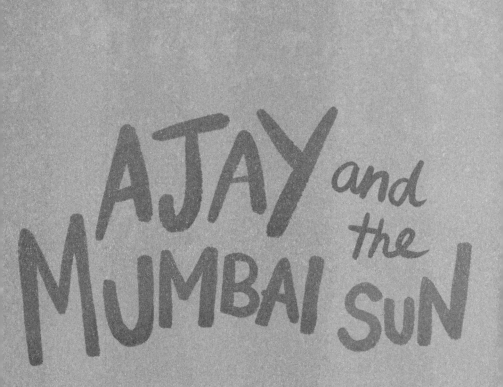

AJAY and the MUMBAI SUN

VARSHA SHAH

Chicken House

SCHOLASTIC INC. / NEW YORK

TO LOU KUENZLER

THE CURRENT AND FORMER STAFF AND STUDENTS
OF KURAYOSHI SOGO SANGYO KYOGO KOKO

FORM 7–10L & 10E1 AND "THE WOMBATS"

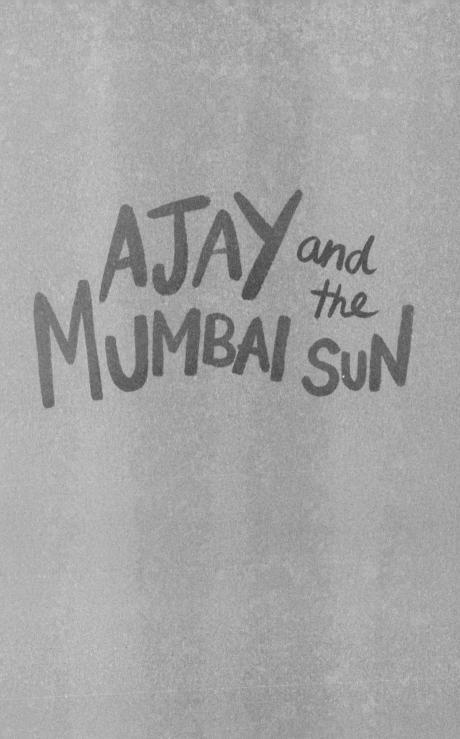

Chapter One

The midafternoon train chugged into Mumbai station.

Ajay grinned even though his stomach was rumbling. He picked up the last newspaper and waved it around like a checkered flag, shouting at the top of his voice: "Ten rupees. Just ten rupees for the latest news. Read all about it!"

A bald businessman with an egg-shaped head and twirly mustache stopped. "How much?"

A customer! Ajay waved the newspaper again. "Ten rupees!"

The businessman looked at him with a crafty glint in his eye. "How do I know the news is worth reading?"

"A lot has happened today," said Ajay.

"Such as?"

Ajay thought quickly back to the early morning at the station, when he had read the newspaper from cover to cover, careful not to damage its creases or stain the crisp, newly minted pages. "An earthquake in Hyderabad."

The businessman shrugged. "That's all?"

"Ten rupees!" said Ajay firmly, holding out his hand.

The businessman pressed his face closer to Ajay's. "Why would I buy a newspaper when you've already told me the main news? Let me give you some free advice. Don't give away anything for free if you want to be successful in this world!"

"But, sir," said Ajay to the man's back, "that's not the most important news."

The man stopped and turned. "What is?"

"A new cure for baldness has been found."

"Let me see that!" The businessman grabbed the newspaper out of Ajay's hand, tearing it as he did so, and rifled through it.

"Where?"

"In the ad section."

"I'm not paying ten rupees for an ad, you scoundrel!"

At that, Ajay drew up to his full height, which was still not much. At twelve—or thereabouts—he still wasn't as tall as the other children abandoned to the railways. He tried to speak with the dignity with which he had seen the station attendant, Niresh, speak to the people he managed.

"I'm not a scoundrel. The newspaper will be ten rupees. Please give it to me at once or I will be forced"—Ajay breathed here, to give time for his words to sink in like sugar cubes in hot chai—"to contact the authorities."

The businessman looked startled. Then his face began to blow up like the cheeks of a fish.

"Are you okay?" Ajay asked, genuinely worried.

The man's mouth opened and closed, his face turning red.

"Why, you grubby little—"

"Is there a problem here?" Niresh came forward from where he had been standing on the platform.

"This filthy thief—" the businessman managed.

"He has taken and read my newspaper, and now will not pay my ten rupees," Ajay cut in patiently.

Niresh looked at Ajay, then at the businessman, then at the paper, and then back at the businessman, and spoke gently. "I am terribly sorry, sahib, but it seems that the boy is right."

"How dare you?" said the businessman, almost apoplectic with anger.

"You're holding the evidence in your hand," said Niresh. "It's the equivalent of a smoking gun. You must pay the boy's ten rupees."

"I will not pay anything. This is a scam!"

Niresh looked at his watch and said again, with his trademark patience, "Of course. That is your choice. We can take a statement, but it will take a few hours and I think your train is in . . . three minutes?"

The businessman looked at the train ready to leave the station, its heavy engine chortling and throwing black dust. People were hanging off its sides and windows. Traders were already running toward it with tiffin boxes clanking, crates of metallic bangles jingling, and bottles of cold lemon water fizzing. A bead of sweat ran down the businessman's face.

"Two minutes," said Ajay helpfully.

"You conniving little railway rat . . ."

"You might need to run," added Niresh with a quick wink at Ajay.

With a noise somewhere between a snarl and a growl, the businessman took out his leather wallet and fished out ten rupees.

"Thank you," said Ajay, beaming.

The businessman looked as if he was fighting the urge to use his briefcase like a golf club.

"Better go now!" said Niresh. "You don't want to miss it."

The businessman started running. He was clearly out of breath.

"Health section is on page five," shouted Ajay, waving.

Chapter Two

The smell of roasted tomatoes and crushed garlic and ginger wafted through the air. Ajay walked up the open platform and breathed it in. It was his lucky day! Nearby, away from the crush of passengers, Vinod, one of the older railway boys—lanky and gentle and, as far as Ajay was concerned, the best cook in Mumbai—was cooking on a small gas canister stove.

"Hey! Vinod!" Ajay called.

"Ajay," Vinod said, looking up. There was a dark bruise on his cheek.

Ajay frowned. "What happened?"

"Nothing."

Ajay didn't ask any more questions, but he found himself clenching his fists. Vinod didn't know, but Ajay had once followed him to find out the cause of those bruises. Through the window of the restaurant where Vinod worked as a cleaner, he had seen Mahesh, the restaurant's owner, cuff Vinod across the face for missing a greasy spot. Ajay had never felt so helpless and had vowed that he would take Mahesh down one day. He repeated the promise to himself now.

"Plate up," said Vinod quietly.

Ajay gave him five rupees—which would not even cover the cost of the ingredients—and took a plate. The curry was smoky and warm and comforting. Vinod was watching him anxiously.

"Is it okay? Not too much salt? Too much chili?"

Ajay slurped appreciatively. "It's good, Vinod! You will be head cook one day." He regretted the words as soon as he said them.

Vinod was a Dalit. Although the law said that he couldn't be discriminated against, Mahesh clearly did just that. He called him "untouchable," of low caste, and wouldn't allow Vinod anywhere near the restaurant food.

Ajay didn't know how to take the words back. He opened his mouth, but Vinod shook his head and changed the subject.

"You know that Mr. Gupta you're always talking about?"

Ajay's eyes shone. Of course he did! Mr. Gupta, the editor of *The City Paper*. His hero. Vinod pushed his glasses up and smiled at Ajay's expression.

"He's going to be at the restaurant tonight. He's made a reservation."

Ajay almost dropped the plate. "Are you sure?"

"Of course I'm sure."

Ajay gulped. Becoming a journalist was the only dream he had ever had.

Vinod looked at him quizzically. "Are you okay?"

Ajay nodded, only half hearing the question. If this was the way to meet Mr. Gupta at last, he had to take it.

Chapter Three

Ajay ran through the market. It was hot, sticky, and crushed with people. He ignored the spice sellers with their scrolls of cinnamon; sneezed as he passed the chili sellers with their vats of ground red powder; and got entangled in fabric as he passed the sari sellers, who had hung their long fabrics of yellow silk on string.

Finally, he made it.

It was his favorite place in the market—the passageway of stationers and booksellers. Shaded from the heat by a gnarled fig tree, it flickered with patches of sunlight that moved with the leaves, but there was no time to explore now. He only had a couple of hours before Mr. Gupta would be at the restaurant.

"Mr. Sandhu!" Ajay cried. "Mr. Sandhu! I want to buy something!"

Mr. Sandhu popped up from behind his stall, the turban wound around his head a bright spot of color. "Ajay. Today is not your birthday, unless I am mistaken?"

Ajay shook his head. He was always at the stall, taking scraps of paper, half-broken bottles of ink, torn pages of magazines—anything that Mr. Sandhu wanted to throw away—but the only time he would actually buy something was his birthday, saving all year to buy just one thing from the stall.

Today wasn't his birthday, but it felt like it should be. Not only one dream, but all his dreams would come true!

"I have a very important commission." He beamed. "I am writing an article for the newspaper." He looked around, then leaned forward to whisper quickly. "Mr. Gupta, the great editor of *The City Paper* himself will be reading it." He leaned back on his heels and continued in his normal voice. "And so, Mr. Sandhu, I need the very best ink that you have."

"The very best?"

"The very best," Ajay confirmed.

"And Ajay." Mr. Sandhu gave a delicate cough. "Will you have any money to pay for this? The very best ink?"

Ajay nodded furiously. "I have seven whole rupees." He had raided his savings. He held them out.

"Seven?" Mr. Sandhu echoed faintly.

Ajay nodded again.

Mr. Sandhu sighed. "Let me look, Ajay." He went inside.

Ajay looked around, full of excitement. The front of the stall was filled with piles of white cartridge paper weighed down with milk-white and pearl conch shells; on the sides were pens—ballpoints, cartridge pens, pens from India, from Germany, from Switzerland—some covered in plastic, some in open velvet boxes; and at the back, paper from all over the world—tissue-thin paper from Japan, silky paper smoothed by shells from Iran, marbled paper from Venice. Ajay snapped back to attention.

"Mr. Sandhu," called Ajay. "I am very sorry, but I am in a rush. Would you be able to hurry?"

Mr. Sandhu popped back up, handing him a glass bottle of black ink.

"Is it satisfactory?" asked Mr. Sandhu.

Ajay held it to his eye like an eyeglass. The ink inside swirled with dark rainbows. He nodded solemnly and handed over the seven rupees—the last of his savings. "Thank you, Mr. Sandhu. And now to write the very important article for Mr. Gupta." He waved and spun round, ready to run back to the station.

And crashed into someone.

Ajay peeled himself from the ground and looked up. It was a man of about forty, who looked like a Bollywood actor, with curly black hair, dark green eyes like ferns in shadow, and razor-sharp cheekbones, in what must have been a very expensive white suit.

Except the white suit was no longer a white suit. The glass stopper on the ink had come loose and the black ink was now covering the man so that he looked like one of the one-hundred-and-one spotted dogs Ajay had seen in the cartoon.

Behind him, he heard Mr. Sandhu say faintly, "Mr. Raz!"

Chapter Four

Ajay felt very bad for this Mr. Raz, but even worse for himself. The ink! It was gone. What was he going to do now? He looked up accusingly at Mr. Raz, his voice filled with bitterness. "Why didn't you look where you were going?"

"Ajay!" Mr. Sandhu sounded a bit breathless.

Mr. Raz's eyebrows shot up, his eyes catching the light from the sun. He took a deep breath, then spoke calmly, his voice sounding rich and mellow, taking the tissues Mr. Sandhu handed to him. "Given that you have just ruined my suit, don't you think that *you* are the one who owes an apology to *me*?"

Ajay stared at him. "You do not understand. I need Mr. Gupta. Mr. Gupta needs an article. The article needs ink." He took a deep breath to keep hold of his panic. "And that ink is now over you." He tried not to despair, but there were only a few hours left! He had to get more ink, but how? "I must go now."

"Not so fast!" said Mr. Raz, grabbing his shoulder.

Ajay felt a sudden stab of fear. The suit did look very expensive. He squirmed, but Mr. Raz's grip was surprisingly strong. Ajay was just about to shout for help when Mr. Raz said, "Do you mean Mr. Gupta the editor of *The City Paper*?"

Ajay nodded as he squirmed.

Mr. Raz looked at him intently. There was the faintest glint of amusement in his green eyes. "You write for the most highly regarded paper in Mumbai?"

Ajay nodded. Then fundamental honesty kicked in. "I *will* write for it. But for Mr. Gupta to know that he must employ me, he has to first read my article." But how could he write his article with no ink?

The glint of amusement disappeared. Mr. Raz let go of Ajay's shoulder. Ajay saw a far-off look in his eye, as if he was remembering a time that was now lost. "There is something about your ambition that reminds me of myself when I was young." He looked down at his white suit, dripping with ink, and sighed. "I hope that I do not regret this. Mr. Sandhu, please give this boy whatever he needs to write his article and charge it to my account."

"The very best of what I need?" said Ajay breathlessly.

"The very best," said Mr. Raz with a laugh. "Sometimes fate works in mysterious ways. A small seed can often, even in the most difficult of conditions, grow into a tree," he said, pointing at the fig tree. "And you can never have enough trees. Now, if you do not mind, I must go home to change." He looked over Ajay's head to the stall owner. "Mr. Sandhu."

"Mr. Raz." Mr. Sandhu nodded.

Ajay and Mr. Sandhu watched Mr. Raz disappear through the crowds. People hurriedly snapped photos of Mr. Raz on their phones as he went past.

Mr. Sandhu looked at Ajay in awe. "Do you know who that is?"

Ajay shook his head.

"He is only Mr. Raz. The great environmentalist. He is an inspiration to us all." Mr. Sandhu stirred himself and in a change of tone said, "Very well, Ajay, what would you like to buy?"

Ajay's eyes widened, hope restored. He rubbed his hands together in glee.

Chapter Five

Ajay ran up the twisted turret of the station, clutching the crystal bottle of ink and the five sheets of white cartridge paper he had gotten from Mr. Sandhu. He ducked under the bit of tape and around the sign that read, NO ENTRY! VERY SCARY! BIG HOLE!!!!! (noting that he would need to repaint it so that it looked new), and crawled in through the open doorway that was only just Ajay's height.

He sneezed. The gold afternoon light came in through the circular tower windows. His room! Not big enough to lie down in, and too hot in the day and too cold at night, but the one place where he could be quiet and write. He had found it in the station when he was about ten years old, scrambling up and up the stone stairs—the only one of the railway kids who loved heights.

The station clock chimed, loud and sonorous.

Hearing it through the floor, Ajay let the paper tumble onto his makeshift desk (two upside-down crates with a wooden board balanced on top), placed the crystal bottle of ink carefully on top, and sat down, flushed with excitement. He had paper! He had ink! (Bright purple to make it memorable.) He had his mother's fountain pen!

And now, thanks to Mr. Raz, he had his story.

Sighing with happiness, Ajay started to write, scratching

the story down with his pen. Halfway through he frowned, got up, stretched, sat down, and opened his scrapbook.

He loved the scrapbook. His friend Yasmin had made it for him from the bits and pieces of paper he had collected from rubbish bins. It must have taken her hours to stitch them together with invisible threads, using cut pieces of material from the factory where she worked to make a cover. In it he had stuck all his favorite articles, carefully cutting them out and pasting them with his pot of glue and brush, his hands covered in newspaper ink.

He opened it up now, the paper crackling between his hands. Inside were his favorite editorials from Mr. Gupta; restaurant reviews from "The Canary" (the most famous food critic in Mumbai); stories of India's cricket team; and, sandwiched in among them, photos. He was right! He had seen Mr. Raz before. There were photos of Mr. Raz in his white suit getting prizes and awards for his environmental work all over the world, and alongside them long articles with flattering quotes from politicians and businessmen and celebrities. Ajay gathered together all the material and wrote his article.

Each hour, the station clock chimed.

The angle of the sun turned and lowered.

On the third chime, Ajay looked up, glowing. It was done! His article on Mr. Raz, summing up what he had found from the pieces in the scrapbook and including his own encounter with him that afternoon, was complete. It had a title too: "The Fig Tree and the Man in the White T!" (Not quite a white suit, but headlines were there to catch attention.)

He felt like jumping. Unable to contain his excitement, Ajay clambered up on top of a crate and pushed open the curved paneled windowpane. Sticking his head out of the window, he looked down. Even the rich people who stayed at the Taj wouldn't be getting such a view! In the low evening light, Mumbai lay spread below him—thrumming: people rushing around like ants, the fringe tops of green-black palm trees swaying like pipe cleaners, the silvery skyscrapers glittering like mirrors as they cut the sky, the patch of lime green that was the cricket ground lying like a postage stamp, the traffic roaring and honking. Soon, everyone in Mumbai would pick up a copy of their newspaper and see his article! He basked in the image for a moment, then rocked back from the window, biting his lip, slowly taking Mother's fountain pen from behind his ear. The black scrolled barrel with its golden nib, which glinted as it caught the last of the day's sunlight, was the only thing that he had of hers; it had been left with him when he'd been abandoned on the railway platform.

A sudden gust of wind came in, whooshing the papers off the desk.

Ajay hurriedly closed the window, scrambled down, and picked up the scattered papers. There was no time to waste. His article was ready and now all he had to do was give it to Mr. Gupta.

Chapter Six

Ajay ran, clutching the article. He couldn't be late! This might be his only chance to meet Mr. Gupta. It was early evening and Mumbai was filled with the sound of horns blaring and people arguing, laughing, chatting, and drinking. Women in silk-shot saris and glittering in fiery rubies and luminescent pearls were stepping out of sleek chauffeur-driven cars. Lights, white and fluorescent, blazed out of late-opening shops and restaurants.

The lights of the restaurant where Vinod worked were different. They gave out a golden glow, signifying how exclusive it was. Ajay quickly looked through the window and took a deep breath when he saw Mr. Gupta, his leathery face familiar from the photo that went above the editorials. He was sitting on his own, apart from the other customers, eating quickly, the sweat running from his brow and down the sides of his face. Ajay ran around to the back of the restaurant and slipped through the iron door into the kitchen.

It took him a while to find Vinod among the bustle of cooks and waiters.

"Vinod!" Ajay whispered.

Vinod turned from the area that he was mopping and waved at Ajay to come inside.

"Mr. Gupta's still here. You've got about half an hour before

Mahesh comes back," Vinod said quietly, after checking that no one had noticed them.

Ajay nodded. "I'll return the favor, Vinod bhai."

"Just don't get caught."

Ajay breathed deeply and went into the main restaurant area, avoiding the eyeline of the waiters, suddenly realizing the article he was holding was creased. Surely Mr. Gupta would see his talent anyway and allow him onto the paper? He made his way to the table. He could only just see above it. Mr. Gupta didn't notice him but continued to eat his curry.

"Mr. Gupta," Ajay said. The words came out as a quiet squeak. Mr. Gupta kept on eating. Ajay cleared his throat and tried again. "Mr. Gupta!"

This time the words came out as a shout. Mr. Gupta dropped his spoon and looked around him, his black brows knitting together furiously.

Ajay coughed and Mr. Gupta looked down at him.

It was now or never. "Mr. Gupta. I am Ajay. I want to work at your paper."

Mr. Gupta's eyes bulged in shock. He didn't say anything, which Ajay took as a good sign.

Ajay plowed on. "I want to be a reporter. You can't make me one now, I know that. But I'll do any job to start—I can clean, or make tea, or do errands. Just let me work for the newspaper. I will find a way to climb up."

"Who are you? And how did you find me here?"

Ajay thought about lying but decided against it. Mr. Gupta was a journalist and would know a lie when he was told one.

"My friend works here. He saw your name on the reservation list."

"You want to work? At the newspaper?" Mr. Gupta repeated blankly.

Ajay nodded. It was all he had ever wanted, the only dream he had ever had. How could he tell Mr. Gupta that? His earliest memories were of sleeping under newspapers for warmth on the station platform. He had learned how to read from newspapers, hoarding each new word like a jewel. At night, when the child-snatchers were at their most predatory and dangerous, Ajay had kept himself awake by reciting headlines. Now all he wanted was to be a reporter. All Mr. Gupta had to do was give him a chance.

Mr. Gupta took a gulp of lime water from the glass by his side. It seemed to cool him down. He turned to Ajay, his eyebrows drawing together. "I can't help you."

Ajay felt his heart stop. "Please—sir . . . I . . ."

Mr. Gupta shook his head. "How old are you anyway? Ten? You should be at school."

Ajay shook his head. How could he tell Mr. Gupta that he needed to work, selling newspapers to survive?

"I'm fourteen," he lied.

"I don't want to hear any more of this," snapped Mr. Gupta. "Don't you know what is happening to newspapers? Offer you a job? Ha! I may not have a job myself much longer. Nobody wants to read papers when they can just look at their phones. Now leave me in peace! I want to finish eating."

Ajay's jaw set. He had to try to make Mr. Gupta understand. "Please, sir. Give me a chance. Read this. It's an article I've written about the great environmentalist Mr. Raz, who I met today." He held up the piece of paper that he'd been holding all this time and had now crumpled in his hand.

Mr. Gupta looked at him, his eyes piercing. But before he could say anything, Ajay felt the article snatched out of his hand. He whipped around, only to face Mahesh, the owner of the restaurant. He must have come back early!

"What is this?" said Mahesh, an ugly sneer in his voice. "A street runt is bothering you in my restaurant? My sincere apologies, Mr. Gupta." He looked at the article that he had snatched from Ajay's hand and started to laugh. "Scribbles on a scrap of paper? Pretending that you have met Mr. Raz!"

Ajay felt himself turn hot with embarrassment and shame. "It's mine. Give it back to me!" he said.

Suddenly, the laughter stopped. Staring at him, Mahesh deliberately tore the article into tiny shreds.

"Stop!" Ajay cried out, trying to gather the bits of paper.

"There's no need for that!" said Mr. Gupta, rising to his feet angrily.

"Who does this kid think he is?" said Mahesh. "Journalists come from Elphinstone College or Churchill School, not the slums!" He gripped Ajay's arm so tightly it hurt. "You're coming with me!"

Mr. Gupta's voice cut through the restaurant. "Enough, Mahesh. Put the boy down—now!"

Mahesh looked as if he was going to ignore him. But then he seemed to realize that the other customers were looking at him as well.

"I said now, Mahesh."

Mahesh slowly released Ajay.

Mr. Gupta turned to Ajay, his eyes filled with regret. "I'm sorry—I wish things were different, but at the moment the newspaper is not doing well. We're firing people, not hiring. I have nothing for you."

Mahesh laughed again, even more harshly than before. "As if a street kid could ever write something worth reading!" The other customers started joining in the laughter.

Ajay felt tears prick his eyes. He forced them back, raised his head high, and looked Mahesh directly in the eye. "One day I will write something worth reading. You'll see." And then he ran out of the restaurant, weaving past the customers who were still laughing and pointing at him as if he were a circus act provided for their entertainment. He wanted to get away before the tears started to fall down his face.

Chapter Seven

The next morning at daybreak, his stomach full from a warm cup of milky chai, Ajay felt better. One day he would show Mahesh, and Mr. Gupta too.

He walked to the part of the city where the printing presses operated, so that he could collect the papers for the day. He scrunched his nose. From inside the iron-barred gates he could hear the clanking and banging and hissing of the printing presses as they worked, and he imagined the papers flying off the presses, hot with newspaper ink.

"You're late!" said the foreman.

"Not that late!" replied Ajay.

The foreman looked as if he was about to make a sharp comment, but stopped as a shout came from behind him.

"Watch out!" Two men were pushing a trolley. On it was a large machine, with a wheel attached to the side.

"What's that?" asked Ajay, curious.

"None of your business!" said the foreman. "Now take those newspapers and go. And remember, on Sunday you will need to bring more money if you want more newspapers to sell."

Ajay grimaced. "Don't remind me!"

He took the pile of newspapers, tied together with brown twine, and carried it in his arms, making sure that it was balanced so that it would not slip from his hands and become dirty. No one would pay for mud-caked papers, no matter how good—or rather, bad—the news.

He saw the two men push the trolley with the large machine out of the printers, take it to the middle of the road, and then dump it. They didn't need to take it to the rubbish pit; they knew that within twenty-four hours it would be stripped by the street kids for scrap metal that they could sell for food.

Ajay sauntered over, still holding the pile of newspapers. "What's that machine?"

The men looked grumpy and fierce, but one, taking note of the newspapers in Ajay's arms, asked, "You're one of the station kids?"

"One and the same!"

The man shook his head but seemed to take pity on him. "It's one of the first printing presses for our newspaper. Hasn't been used for decades. The new owner of the paper saw it and told us to get rid of it. A shame. A piece of history thrown into the street." He shrugged. "I'm getting sentimental. Should worry about my own job rather than a piece of metal." He nodded, then left with the other man to go back into the printing rooms.

Ajay looked at the machine in front of him. It was made of iron and looked rusted and damaged. He should leave it there. It was no good to anyone except for its scrap value. He turned to go . . .

. . . then turned back again.

The printing press stood there, solid and heavy and reliable. Despite the rust and damage, it looked well made. A press that someone had taken care and time over making. A press that could even now create a newspaper . . .

Ajay ran as fast as he could, back to the railway station.

Chapter Eight

"I can't believe you made me come out here!" Saif said grumpily to Ajay. They were pushing one of the trolleys used to carry luggage by the porters on the first-class trains down the street.

"Hurry up! We need to get there quickly!"

"'Hurry up!' he says. It doesn't matter that I've got to get up early tomorrow to help the chief engineer. It doesn't matter that I've worked all day fixing the engine of the express train and am covered in oil. It doesn't matter that I was just getting ready to eat the fried pakoras I've been saving for dinner when . . . Ahhh."

Saif stopped and stared.

They had gotten to where the printing press sat still in the pale early morning light, as if it had been waiting for them.

"Now do you see?" said Ajay, bursting with pride. "Aren't you happy that I woke you?"

Saif said nothing. He just stood, staring at the machine in front of him with large, wonder-filled eyes. Then he stepped forward reverently and looked at it from all angles.

"Is it what I think it is?"

"A printing press," said Ajay wisely, "with metal plates, type, and presses. I believe it is a hundred years old." He had nothing to base that on, except for the fact that it didn't seem to run on electricity, but it sounded good.

"I think you're right," whispered Saif.

"I am?" said Ajay, astonished. Then he recovered. "Of course I am! I am always right! The question is, what do we do now?"

"We take it back, of course!" said Saif, still whispering, as if he were talking about a mythical phoenix rather than a printing press. "I will get it working again. I will show the railway engineers that I am not just good for cleaning machine parts!"

"Of course!" said Ajay, but he felt his enthusiasm dampen as he looked at the machine. It looked bigger than he remembered.

They both pushed at it. Then again.

"Ow!" Saif rubbed his arms. "It's hopeless! I am an apprentice engineer. I am not a weightlifter. I am not made for this!"

Ajay leaned back against the machine, sweating. "If it comes to it, Saif, I am not sure I'm made for this either—but we've got to try!"

He looked around, then spotted a huge metal pole. "That's it!"

It felt like it took hours, but eventually, by using the pole as a lever, they got it on the trolley and to the station—to the engine room at the back of the building where the broken railway engines were kept.

"Are you sure you can fix it, Saif?"

"Of course!" said Saif, blowing his cheeks and chest up pompously. Then he looked at Ajay suspiciously. "Why?"

Ajay grinned. "Why else? We're going to create our very own newspaper!"

Saif's stomach and cheeks deflated slowly, like balloons that had their air let out. "You've gone mad. Those books you keep picking up from the garbage bins have made you lose all your sense. Who'll want to read a newspaper by railway kids?"

For a moment Ajay felt downcast, then he rallied. "Everyone!"

Saif looked at him in disbelief.

Ajay gave in a little. "We just need to make them realize it."

Chapter Nine

As he sold the day's newspapers at the platform, Ajay planned.

A newspaper needed three things: an editor (Ajay beamed; he was made for that role); content—printed, not "scribbles on scraps of paper"; and pictures. He frowned—where could he get pictures from? It was only at the end of the day, when the sky turned blue-black like a peacock's tail, that Ajay suddenly snapped his fingers.

He checked the clock at the station. There was still time. To get to the factory he had to pass through the outskirts of the slum that was made up of shelters of cardboard and corrugated iron. As Ajay weaved his way through, he saw men gathering in groups; cats arching their backs and hissing, waiting for scraps of food; kids coming back home from the rubbish dumps where they had been looking for pieces of scrap metal. Finally, he got to the newly built textile factory, where the doorways were edged in lamplight. He pushed open the door and poked his head around. In the enormous room, huge rollers were pressing through sheets of material, worked by young people, their scrawny arms flexing under the weight; and vats of dyes were being stirred, the bright saffron-orange and vermilion-red liquids slopping out of their containers. Ajay could barely hear himself think with the chugging and creaking sounds of the machinery all around him. But then he spotted Yasmin concentrating on the fabric in front of her.

He went to her and waited until she had pressed the wooden block, carved into an intricate pattern of mangoes, into a turquoise dye and then pressed it into the pink material in front of her. It left behind a print that linked with other identical prints into a precise chain, creating a pattern for the T-shirt. The fumes from the dyes were making his stomach churn.

"Yasmin!"

She looked up blankly, her concentration broken. Then she saw him, and grimaced. "What are you doing here?"

"I've come to make you an offer."

Yasmin just looked at him skeptically. She was also about twelve. They'd met in the slums, where she lived, when she had beaten up one of the boys bothering him.

"I want you to create designs for my newspaper."

"Your newspaper?"

Ajay nodded. "I have a newspaper. I need someone to help design it and create a title design."

"What are you talking about?"

Ajay looked at her impatiently. "Designs for a newspaper. I need someone to draw them. Will you do it?"

Yasmin's green eyes opened wide. She became very still.

Just at that moment, one of the older ladies working at the prints screeched at her. "What are you doing? Who is this? Get back to work! We're already two T-shirts behind thanks to your chattering!"

Yasmin blinked as if she had been woken up from a dream.

Ajay looked at the two security guards coming toward him.

They hooked an arm through each of his and dragged him out of the building.

"Think about what I said!" shouted Ajay to Yasmin.

The guards threw him onto the cold concrete outside with dire warnings of what would happen to him if he returned. Ajay picked himself up and shook the dust off the shoulders of his T-shirt. One day he would be wearing one of those spick-and-span suits that he had seen people wear on the railways when they were taking important phone calls, or maybe even a white suit like Mr. Raz.

"Ajay!"

Ajay looked around.

"Over here!" Yasmin was at the door, a desperate look in her eyes. "Did you mean it?"

"Mean what?"

"That I could draw my own designs? That I wouldn't have to use other people's patterns? That I could draw them myself?" Her eyes were still wide and she was shaking as if his answer meant the world to her.

"Yes," said Ajay, smiling.

"Then I'm in." She turned and went back inside, her hair swirling behind her.

Ajay stood there and closed his eyes for a moment. He couldn't quite believe his dream was beginning to come true.

Chapter Ten

"Well?" said Saif, a week later. "Aren't you impressed with the work I've done? It is not for nothing that I'm an apprentice engineer."

Ajay looked over the printing press. He *was* impressed. Saif had cleaned and oiled it, and taken it apart and put it back together again, until it sat there squat, sparkling, and silvery.

"Does it work?"

Saif looked as if Ajay had just wounded him. "You dare ask if it works? Do I look like someone who would do something for show? Look at this." Saif pointed at the silver plates of metal. "This is where you put the paper." He pressed the lever. "This is what makes the paper go through the press." He showed Ajay the tiles. "And this is where the iron letter pieces go that print the paper."

Ajay breathed slowly, trying to keep the excitement inside rather than let it explode like a firecracker.

"Now all you need is the stories!" Saif looked around, as if the stories were like elephants and just about to walk in. "Where are they?"

Ajay felt his excitement dampening a little. It wasn't anyone else's fault. Vinod had agreed to create recipes for the food section of the paper; Yasmin had already carved a block of wood with the words *The Mumbai Sun*—and the design of a sunburst and a scrolled interlocking pattern of trains and arches; Saif had gotten the printer working. Everyone had done their part. Now it was up to him. He had to write the first story.

"Well?" asked Saif again.

Ajay thought hard. The first story had to have drama, excitement, tension—it had to be an exclusive. And he had no idea what it could be—but he would. "It will be ready, Saif! Just make sure the printers are ready to roll."

"Haven't you forgotten something?"

"What?"

"We need paper and ink."

Compared to finding stories, that's a piece of paratha, thought Ajay, his stomach rumbling at the thought of the fried doughy bread. "Leave it to me, Saif."

After selling the day's newspapers, Ajay went to his favorite place in all of Mumbai to think. The Hanging Gardens were green and fresh and filled with moisture. He sat on a bench. He thought about the slum, the factory, the railway station— all the millions of people who lived in Mumbai. What would make them pick his newspaper to read? He needed a story that was important, something that the newspaper could campaign on, something that would make people care. It shouldn't take more than five minutes for him to come up with an idea—after all, he was Ajay the newspaperman. He always had plenty of ideas!

Chapter Eleven

Five hours later, he was still thinking . . .

Why were the ideas not coming? He always had so many of them! The shadows around the gardens were deepening into blues as deep as the sapphires worn by the wealthy women in the center of the city. Ajay counted to a hundred and back again. He did yoga poses like the priests at the temple by the station. He walked around in circles with his hands behind his back, whistling. It was no good. Nothing worked! No matter what he tried, no ideas came into his head. Mahesh's words echoed in his mind—*As if a street kid could ever write something worth reading!* Ajay felt his face scrunch up in despair. What if Mahesh was right?

Dejected, Ajay walked back toward the railway, his head hung low. He was walking through the shadows of the slum, with its ramshackle dwellings and maze of paths, when a sharp cry shattered the air. He ran toward the sound. A pack of men were there, among the dwellings, looking like jackals itching for a fight. Some were holding heavy metal bars in their hands; others, with sacks and hammers, were pinning notices on wooden posts. Ajay felt a bolt of fear, knowing that the smart thing to do would be to disappear. These men would not care if they broke boxes or bodies. As he watched, the biggest of them all, a brute with red eyes and a belly that hung over his trousers, shoved an old, bearded man to the ground.

"Interfere again, slum-rat, and I'll beat you till you turn black and blue!" he said, showing a gold tooth in his mouth filed to a sharp edge.

"But this is our home! What are you doing here? What's on the notices?" said the old man. Ajay's mouth fell open at the man's bravery.

"I won't tell you again—what's on the notices is not your business," said the man with the golden tooth, his tone menacing as he stepped nearer. The pack of men who were pinning notices were taking photos of them by the light of oil lamps and then tearing down the same notices before putting them in the sacks.

Other people from the slum had gathered, watching the men, frozen into silence.

Ajay straightened his back. He was now a newspaper editor; he had to do something. It was his job to help the powerless! What affected one, affected all. He searched his pocket. There was almost always something useful that he had stored in there. Surely there would be now as well? He found a glass bead. That would do it!

"Look! I've found a diamond from a woman's necklace!" he crowed.

One of the men almost dropped his camera. "Give me that!"

"I'm in charge here," growled the man with the golden tooth, turning to them. "It belongs to me!"

Ajay made his voice sound as small and pleading as he could. "That is my diamond!" From the corner of his eye he watched as a girl quickly stepped forward to help the old man up and draw him back into the shadows. The crowd had melted away to safety.

"You're going to say no to me?" The man with the golden tooth grinned, his eyes flashing. He grabbed Ajay's wrist, his hand like a vise, squeezing until Ajay yelped in pain. Taking the bead, he went over to one of the oil lamps, his eyes flickering with greed. All the other men went there too, staring at the bead he was holding and muttering among themselves. Ajay quickly clambered up on an upturned wooden crate, tore the notice down, and pocketed it. There must be a reason why the men were taking photos of it and then hiding it. Just in time. The man with the golden tooth turned around, an ugly expression on his face. "This is not a diamond. It's glass. Why, you stupid—"

"My mistake!" said Ajay. He edged away, still nursing his bruised wrist. The man bared his teeth and then, looking as if it was too much trouble to deal with Ajay, turned back to the now-empty post.

Ajay heard the stream of curses behind him. But it was too late. Ajay had made his escape with the notice in his pocket, running as quickly as he could through the dark passageways of the slum.

He didn't stop running until he got to his room at the railway station, where, with trembling hands, he lit a small lamp with a match and by the glowing light read the notice that the thugs were so desperate to keep secret from the people of the slum. His eyes widened. On the notice was written: *Slums to be demolished in one month's time. All buildings in the area to be destroyed. Any concerns to be raised within seven days.*

People were going to lose their homes, and unless he did something they would not realize it until it was too late.

Almost without thinking, he took out his mother's fountain pen.

He spent all night in his room writing, forgetting the pain in his wrist, forgetting everything around him. The glow from the oil lamp threw out pools of light as he scribbled down the article, scratching out words here and there and rewriting whole sentences with a spatter of inkblots. When he was done, he blew the ink dry and ran his fingers through his hair, bursting with excitement. He had his first real story—one that he had investigated himself—and it was ready to go to press!

Chapter Twelve

At dawn, Yasmin and Saif, rubbing the sleep out of their eyes, met Ajay in front of the station. Vinod was already there, sprinkling loose brown tea leaves that Yasmin had bought for them into an earthenware pot filled with milk. The editorial team was ready for action, and in front of them was a pile of the very first issue of *The Mumbai Sun*!

Ajay puffed out his chest with pride. They had done it. They had spent all night cranking the printing press, folding the pages inside one another, and stamping each one on top with the title.

They had produced a real newspaper!

"See, my friends. See what we have made! Like the sun itself, it will provide light! It will provide hope! It will be the best newspaper in Mumbai!"

Saif looked at him doubtfully. "But it doesn't *look* like a newspaper. What do you think, Vinod?"

Vinod looked up from where he was adding cardamom and cinnamon bark to the tea-infused milk and boiling it until the mixture bubbled furiously. "The newspaper is very pink," he said eloquently, then turned back to concentrate on the tea. Vinod rarely spoke, but when he did, his words counted.

Ajay felt his chest deflate. Strictly speaking, Saif and Vinod were right. Finding paper had been harder than Ajay thought.

He'd had to resort to using the paper from the packaging factory, which was undeniably a shade of faluda-milkshake pink. Then he perked up—after all, newspapers were there to be noticed, and who could avoid looking at a rose-pink paper with blue print? (The ink was made from a mixture of one part leftover ink to eight parts blue dye from the T-shirt factory.)

"People don't just want stories that are black and white, they want color! With the paper we have used, they will know our newspaper is full of color," he said confidently to the others.

Vinod stayed tactfully silent, taking the pot of tea and pouring the caramel-colored liquid from a height into another pot and then back again, until it frothed and smelled of warmth and spices.

"Are you sure about this?" said Yasmin, her emerald eyes searching his. He opened his mouth to defend the pink paper, and she impatiently shook her head. "Not that. Are you sure about printing the story about the notice? The men who you stole it from are dangerous—and it's to do with people in the slum, like me. You live here, in the railway—you don't have to get involved. You could keep selling the other newspapers instead like you did before."

"The pen—and print—is mightier than the sword," said Ajay solemnly. "They were trying to hide the notices about tearing down the slum. People must know what they are up to."

Yasmin nodded, the anger at the men destroying her home clear in her stance.

"What I still don't understand," said Saif, scratching his head, "is why they were taking photos of the notices before taking them down."

Yasmin cut in impatiently. "That's easy. They have to pretend to the judges that they told everyone about the slum clearance, so the men put the notices up and take photos as proof, then they tear them down before anyone has a chance to actually read them."

Ajay nodded. "Exactly. And now these men will be brought to justice! It is time, my friends, for us to distribute the paper. Take a pile each and give one to everyone you meet. Vinod—glasses, please . . ."

Vinod added a generous helping of sugar to the tea and gave it, in cups he'd fashioned out of red clay, to Ajay and the others, keeping one for himself. Ajay held his in front of him. The steam curled up his nose. "To the newspaper!" he cried.

"The newspaper," said Yasmin, still blazing with anger at the men.

"The newspaper," said Vinod steadily.

"The newspaper!" cried Saif, excitement suddenly overcoming him.

They hit their cups together, splashing the liquid down the sides and gulping down what was left of the fragrant drink.

Ajay had never felt as happy in his life. It was the first day of *his* newspaper—a newspaper that would change the world!

Chapter Thirteen

Five hours later and Ajay felt his jubilant mood vanish like the dregs of the chai slipping through a sieve.

No one had taken the newspaper seriously.

Businessmen had stormed past, whacking him with their briefcases; elderly women had grabbed the faluda-pink paper for a couple of coins—but then used it to wrap their fried dough balls stuffed with lentils and coconut and raisins; children had run into the pile, kicking it and causing the sheaves of paper to fly into the air like pink paper kites. Ajay had run this way and that, snatching at the sheets before they caught in the wind. He sat down on the platform steps, his brow furrowed, his eyes hot. Why did no one want his newspaper? It had everything—color (bright pink), recipes (samosas with green chili pickle), and story ("The slum-clearing thug with the golden tooth")—but no one wanted it. How could he change the world with his words if no one cared?

Ajay heard Saif's familiar huffing as he climbed up to the platform. He looked up hopefully, but Saif—panting—was lugging back all the papers he had taken to sell. Vinod, coming from the direction of the rail tracks, had all his papers as well. He shook his head gently. Yasmin came running, her black hair flying around her, holding her pile. She slammed it down on to the ground, her green eyes flashing.

"It's no good," she said. "No one cares. No one wants to know what happens in the slum. It was all for nothing."

Ajay saw her wipe away a tear furiously, trying to hide it from him.

He stood up, his own doubts vanishing. That would not do! He would be strong and courageous for her, like the warrior Tipu Sultan. He drew himself up with dignity.

"Do not worry. I have a plan to sell these papers."

Saif looked at him. "Well? What is it? And why did you not tell us it before? I am an apprentice engineer. My time is valuable! Trains depend on me to run." He crossed his arms, glaring at Ajay.

Vinod looked at him quietly, expectantly.

"Well," said Ajay, playing for time. "All we need to find is a selling point. What is it that everyone in India cares about? More than anything else?"

Saif scowled as he tried to think.

Yasmin bit her lip.

But it was Vinod who spoke. "Cricket."

He said nothing else, but that one word electrified Ajay, Saif, and Yasmin.

"Cricket," repeated Ajay, nodding sagely and trying to hide his excitement.

Saif looked from Ajay to Vinod and back again, then uncrossed his arms. "I don't understand. How does that help us? We don't play cricket, we can't afford to go and watch it, and we have nothing to do with it."

Ajay grinned as a plan began to form in his head. "That doesn't matter, brother Saif. We're not stumped yet! In fact, I have an idea that might just get us past this sticky wicket. An idea that will bowl everyone over . . ."

Yasmin rolled her eyes.

Chapter Fourteen

It was early evening in the slum. Saif, Vinod, and Yasmin were all at work. Ajay would have to do this part of the plan on his own.

He slipped through the winding passages that led to the heart of the slum, threading his way through the shacks made of corrugated iron and pieces of wood boarded together, that leaned against one another like pieces in a game of carrom. Old dogs were yapping and growling as they snuffled for food from their owners. Ajay shivered—he was not on his home turf. At the railway station there were many orphans like him, but here, grandmothers were flicking chapatis on smoky open fires for their grandsons, and women were returning from backbreaking work to hug their daughters. He felt a prickle at the back of his throat. If the slum was built over, it wouldn't just be buildings and homes that would be destroyed; it would be entire families. He didn't have a family, but he would protect those who did. He had to get people to read his newspaper and realize how much danger the slum—and everyone in it—was in.

At last he got to the center of the slum and the narrow rectangular lamplit courtyard. A group of boys were playing cricket there. Ajay had been watching them play cricket for months— every chance he could get. He'd always done it from the shadows—the boys were older and tougher than him, and would squash him if they got a chance. Jai, a tall boy of about fifteen, was at the wall, holding a makeshift bat made from a finely sanded plank of wood. He looked scrawny, but with a wiry toughness that was clear in the way he stood and held the bat.

A ball was bowled.

Ajay watched as Jai hit it with a resounding thwack. The ball shot through the air and hit a corrugated roof in the distance. A six! The highest score of runs possible from a single ball.

Slum kid or not, Ajay was willing to bet that Jai was one of the best batsmen in Mumbai.

He squared his shoulders—it was now or never—and stepped into the light: "Mr. Jai!"

Jai turned to face him slowly. His eyes were the golden color of clarified butter, their warmth offset by the cynical twist of his mouth. He looked down at Ajay, speaking softly.

"What do you think you are doing interrupting our game?"

The other kids crowded around. They were all a foot taller than Ajay and spoiling for a fight. Ajay swallowed his fear. "Mr. Jai! Listen to me. I would only interrupt you on a matter of great importance. You have clear talent. I want to do a feature— to showcase your talent across India."

"Who is this kid?" said a boy with a broken nose from the crowd, threateningly.

"One of the railway boys!" answered another. "Let's show him what it means to come to our area alone!"

"You heard it, kid. Get lost before you get hurt," said Jai, his voice losing none of the softness.

Ajay shook his head sadly. "I am sorry, Mr. Jai. I cannot do that. You see, you have to let me help you. If you don't—none of this"—Ajay took a moment to wave his hand to encompass the courtyard and the slum buildings surrounding it—"will exist for much longer."

Jai raised an eyebrow. "What are you talking about?"

"I am the editor of a newspaper."

There was a snigger from the crowd. Ajay ignored it and plowed on. "We have a breaking story. The slum is going to be demolished, but people don't want to read about that—they want to read about sportsmen."

Jai looked at him incredulously for a moment. "What do you mean the slum is going to be cleared? And what do I have to do with that?"

Ajay held his gaze, hoping that his nerves weren't showing. "A sportsman has power both on the pitch and off it."

When he didn't say anything more, Jai spoke again. "You—think I am that? A sportsman? You must be crazy!"

"Am I?" Ajay challenged him. "Don't you want to play against the top private school in the country and show that you are better than any of the boys there?"

A look of longing passed across Jai's face. Just as quickly, it was gone, and the cynical twist of his mouth grew more bitter. "Get lost, before I throw you out myself."

As some of the other boys pressed closer, Ajay spoke desperately. "Listen to me! I can make it happen—for all of you. And if you agree, I'll be able to get people to read my newspaper—and then save the slum. But you have to agree first!"

Jai looked at him. "I'm not a sportsman, kid. I beg for food, get kicked in the stomach, and am spat on—every—single—day. I have to put up with all of it to get a few measly rupees. And you think I can become a sportsman?"

"You don't have to become one. You are already a sportsman! Just like I'm a newspaper editor."

The others laughed.

But Jai took a sudden breath and looked at Ajay as if seeing him for the first time. Ajay counted to himself to keep calm, "One kachori, two kachori, three . . ." There was a long pause. Finally, Jai spoke. "What exactly do you want me to do?"

Ajay grinned.

The next morning, Jai was standing by Ajay on the platform in bright cricket whites that Ajay had gathered from the station's lost property office and were too short for him, looking distinctly uncomfortable, as Ajay waved his newspaper. An extra front page had been attached to the previous day's copies. "Read all about it! The diamond in the rust. The boy who private schools are afraid of! The boy who could bat for India if only he was given a chance! Read his exclusive full story here in *The Mumbai Sun!*"

Businessmen stopped checking the cricket scores on their phones to buy copies of the paper; elderly women stopped to read the papers they bought, before using them as food wrapping; and children tried to make out the letters of the paper and then hurled themselves toward the pile, only to be picked up by the scruffs of their necks by Jai and placed out of harm's way before they could wreck it.

Ajay sat down at the end of the day, exhausted, but happier

than he had ever been in his life. There wasn't a single copy of the newspaper left, and the only two things being discussed at the station were the cricket team from the slums that terrified the private schools, and the slum itself that was due to be demolished within the month.

Chapter Fifteen

A protestor slammed into Ajay.

"Look here!" said Ajay hotly, trying to turn around. It was hopeless. Another body squashed him from the left, and then another from the right.

"Hey! Watch out!" he tried to shout, but no one noticed. People were marching through the slum to the dusty clearing at its edge, and he was being carried with them like a pebble that had been tossed into the river Ganga. Ajay looked up, trying to take notes with his mother's fountain pen on the half-broken spiral notebook he had recovered from a railway bin. But all he could see were bodies pressed against him from all sides, and clenched fists.

This was no good! He needed to get a better vantage point. He tucked the pen behind his ear, then took a deep breath and dived in between legs and heavy footfalls. He dodged and pushed and scrummed. No one could stop him! He was like one of those rugby players from Japan he'd seen in the papers! But he mistimed one of his dives and a kick sent him somersaulting through the protestors. He landed with a thud on the side of the path.

"Ow!"

With as much dignity as he could muster, Ajay gingerly got up, dusting the soil from his trousers. He felt a flash of envy, like the bite of green chilies, as he saw the crowd part for two journalists in crisp suits and clean shoes, their press passes around their necks. If only he had a press pass!

With the scrum of people and the trees hemming them in, there was no way that he would be able to see anything now.

Unless . . .

He looked at the neem tree next to him and brightened.

Five minutes later, having scrambled up the tree and perched on a branch as close as he could get to the stage, Ajay watched the scene below. An angry group of protestors from the slum had gathered in the square in front of the makeshift podium. To the side were several news reporters. Onstage was Mrs. Shania, the politician for the area, with a beehive hairdo and sharp red painted nails. Ajay felt a thrill of excitement as he leaned forward. He had never seen her in real life before; only on posters that were stuck on every wall with the tag line "Mother of the City." *The Mumbai Sun* must have made an impact to get her to come here! Just like in the posters, she was smiling. The sound system screeched. Ajay licked his pen, turned to a fresh page in his dog-eared notebook, and made himself comfortable on the tree branch, wishing that he had some spiced popcorn to munch on as he watched. Being a newspaperman was hungry work.

Mrs. Shania took the mic, tapping it sharply with one of her red nails. There was a crackle, and then her voice echoed around the square. "I am here because, as a result of false reports in the media, there have been some misunderstandings between you— the people, and us—the people who live to serve you." There was a pause as she looked at them with that smile still on her face. Then she spoke again. "We only have your best interests at heart."

"Are you building over the slum or not?" Jai's blunt words carried across the crowd. He was standing to one side, a cricket ball in one hand and a cool expression on his face.

Mrs. Shania looked irritated for a moment but then smoothed her expression, her voice becoming cloying like sugar syrup. "'Building over' sounds so . . . *destructive*. What we are doing is improving the slums. Getting rid of dangerous, unsafe, and hazardous buildings."

Ajay bounced on the branch. He couldn't help himself. "Excuse me!" Mrs. Shania looked around.

"Over here!" Ajay waved, causing the branch to shake and a few pieces of fruit to fall from the tree, tumbling over the heads of the men in suits.

"Yes?" said Mrs. Shania, her expression still smooth but with a hint of ice in her tone.

"They all mean the same thing."

For a moment she looked stunned. "Excuse me?"

"'Dangerous, unsafe, and hazardous' all mean the same thing," said Ajay helpfully. "Did you mean to add something else?"

"The slum's a deathtrap!" Mrs. Shania snapped. Then, with visible effort, she smiled at the crowd again. "I mean . . . as I was saying. These buildings—these *extremely dangerous* buildings— will be replaced with ones that are modern, safe, and have all the amenities you could wish for. It will be newly built, like the modern textile factory run by Mr. Gir. Now . . ."

Ajay frowned. He needed more factual detail than this to fill up the column inches. He waved again.

Mrs. Shania looked up, her hand gripping clawlike on the mic. "Yes?"

"What amenities?"

"I'm sorry?"

"What amenities?"

"Oh—all of them." She gave an airy laugh that seemed a little forced. "You know . . ."

Ajay felt confused. "No. I don't know. That's why I'm asking."

"I don't think we need to go into details—"

"He means—will there be running water? Indoor toilets? Heating? Lighting? Strong walls?" said Jai, his voice and expression cool but his eyes focused on her with the laser-like intensity he usually kept for untrustworthy bowlers.

Mrs. Shania hesitated. Then, looking at the crowd that was beginning to turn restless, her eyes flickered. "Yes. Of course. The new buildings have been planned to include all the modern amenities."

The crowd cheered. Ajay wrote it all down carefully in his notebook.

"You mean that every single person here will have access to hot water, toilets, heating—all of it?" asked Jai over the noise, hope flaring in his eyes.

"Isn't that what you want? Somewhere to be safe? With everything you need?" asked Mrs. Shania, her voice suddenly turning soft as silk. Ajay looked up with interest. She hadn't actually answered Jai's question.

"Of course that is what the people want, Mrs. Shania," said

one of the journalists. "Only you could give the people what they want, before they even realize they want it!"

The crowd quieted down for a moment, looking uncomfortable as the journalist laughed at his own joke. No one disagreed with Mrs. Shania though. Ajay felt his thoughts wander for a moment as he dreamed of what safety and warmth and shelter would look like. What it would feel like.

Mrs. Shania smiled. "Well then, you should be pleased to know that Mr. Z, one of the richest men in India, if not the world, is entrusted with the building of this great project. When it is finished it will be one of the most modern developments in Mumbai, and when you move to these buildings, you will be building a new life not just for yourselves, but for future generations as well."

Everyone clapped and cheered. Ajay frowned. It sounded so good, but there was something that bothered him. He clicked his fingers as he got it.

"Excuse me!"

"More questions?" Mrs. Shania said, her voice sharp.

Ajay nodded energetically. He was a newspaper editor on assignment. It was his job to ask questions! "What do you mean 'move to these buildings'?"

Mrs. Shania kept staring at him.

"You said 'move to these buildings,' not 'move into.' Where are these new buildings going to be?"

The crowd, like a flurry of fireworks that had suddenly fizzled out, fell silent.

"Shall I repeat the question?" asked Ajay, trying to be helpful again.

"No," said Mrs. Shania coldly. "You do not need to repeat the question. You do not need to worry either. Mr. Z's company is buying up some prime land nearby. The new buildings will be built there."

The crowd looked relieved.

"And that is all for the questions," continued Mrs. Shania. "Does anyone still wish to object?"

No one did. After all, she had just promised that the deepest dreams of every person standing there would come true: homes with running water, toilets, and walls that wouldn't collapse.

"Very well then. The excavators will arrive here in one month's time to clear the slums of these dangerous buildings. As for now, my office has prepared free food for you all. Please help yourselves!"

Ajay felt his mouth water at the delectable smells coming from the food carts. But he hesitated. Everything that Mrs. Shania had said sounded so wonderful. New buildings, modern facilities, prime land! And yet . . . something still rankled. Ajay looked back down at the crowd from the tree.

He caught his breath.

On the edge of the crowd—where only he, from his vantage point in the tree, could see him—was the thug with the gold tooth, and with him, the men who had been putting up the notices of the slum clearance, photographing them, and tearing them down before they could be seen by anyone who lived there. Ajay felt a knot of fear as he saw the burly leader of the three men grin, his golden tooth flashing in the bright sunlight, and was about to shout, cry out a warning to the crowd, anything!

But before he could, as if at a signal, the men melted into the shadows.

Ajay's heart was pounding; his reporter's instinct was on fire. If the plans were really as good as Mrs. Shania said they were, there would have been no need to enlist the gang members.

Something was wrong, and it was up to him as the editor of *The Mumbai Sun* to find out what.

And with the excavators coming into the slums, he had just a month to do it in.

Chapter Sixteen

The rain pattered on the corrugated iron roof of the platform, tap-tap-tapping down in an endless, dreary, silvery stream. Inside one of the side rooms, just next to Niresh's office, the windows were steaming up with the scent of cream and spices. Vinod was smiling gently as he ladled up bowlfuls of bhiriyani: the rice, flecked with saffron and almonds, glistening in the light, and underneath, the fragrant curry with slivers of caramelized onion, cumin-dusted cubes of potato and green beans.

"Happy birthday, Vinod bhai!" said Saif, rubbing his hands—his eyes round with anticipation of the meal. "Being an apprentice engineer is hungry work! This is the sort of food we should have every day, not once a year! We need energy to build such big machines that all of India needs to run on!"

Yasmin rolled her eyes, but even she couldn't help grinning as she stopped testing out a game called Jenga that had been left on a railway train and cleaned up as a present for Vinod. She got up to take her bowl. They had all contributed to Vinod's birthday meal. Ajay had spent two nights cleaning out the spice seller's store in return for five strands of saffron. He took a spoonful and groaned in delight at the spicy warmth of the rice. "You have outdone yourself, Vinod bhai!" And then, because after all he was the editor and an editor must always put his paper first, he added, "You will write up the recipe for the paper?"

Vinod nodded and Ajay settled back, feeling happier. He had written up the story of the press conference, but without more information, and with the majority of the people in the slum in favor of the clearance, there was little to add by way of new stories. It was a slow news week and the chalkboard he had made to count down to the date the excavators came to the slums showed that there were only three weeks left. Investigative work took time, and resources. In the meantime though *The Mumbai Sun* was still doing brisk work: mainly to do with Vinod's recipes (a hit with readers, who were now waiting for each new edition of the paper as if for news of India's space mission); and to do with the profile articles Ajay was doing on Jai—"Cricketer was three when he first hit a ball of chapati dough on the president's nose!" (President of local vegetable collective, not of the US, but that was only clarified in paragraph five.)

Ajay looked at Jai, who was sitting in the corner. In general, Jai still kept himself apart from the rest of the team, but from time to time he would join them unannounced. He had come today, handing Vinod a packet of almonds without a word. Vinod had taken them just as silently, a slight shake of the hand being the only sign of how much the gift from his friend meant to him. Ajay stirred. It was time to find out how far the investigations had gone. He hit the edge of his bowl with a spoon.

"Sorry to interrupt the celebrations, Vinod bhai," he said politely, "but the next edition is due and I need some news. What is the update on our investigations?"

Everyone was silent. They all looked at one another, and then looked at their bowls with determined concentration. Ajay waited. A good editor was patient at all times.

It was taking too long.

"Anyone?"

Finally, Saif spoke up. "I have done some research among the engineers. As you know, we are around very expensive machinery. Much of the machinery is made by Mr. Z's company. It is a big company with many shell companies."

"Shell companies?" asked Vinod.

"That's what one of the engineers told me," said Saif with confidence. "He must be gathering shells from Chowpatty Beach."

Everyone looked confused. If there was so much money to be made from collecting shells, why wasn't everyone doing it? Ajay shrugged. It was another question to investigate.

"Anything else?" he asked Saif.

Saif nodded, clearly in his element. "He is India's biggest Bollygarch."

"What's a Bollygarch?"

"The engineer told me. *B* is for Bombay. An oligarch is part of a small group of people who hold all the power. So Mr. Z is part of the group that holds all the power here!" Saif grinned from ear to ear, proud of his deduction.

Ajay frowned. "But Bombay is called Mumbai now! Why don't we call him a Mollygarch?"

"Because it doesn't sound as scary?" suggested Vinod.

Ajay tested out both versions in his head. Yasmin interrupted his thoughts. "But why don't we hear more about him? Who exactly is he?" she said.

Ajay shook his head. He had looked through his scrapbook. There were no pictures of Mr. Z anywhere.

Jai supplied the information on that one. "They said that he spends most of his time in London."

"Why?" asked Yasmin.

"They said that there are some people there who like Bollygarchs and—in return for money—protect them from prosecution."

"Wait a minute—who's 'they'?" asked Ajay, proud to remember the rule from the journalism films: Always check your source!

Jai looked uncomfortable. "Two lawyers talking in the street."

There was a moment of silence. Ajay felt his face turn hot. He shouldn't have asked. Jai felt embarrassed about begging in the streets when the rest of the team all had jobs.

All at once, Ajay frowned. Jai shouldn't have to feel embarrassed! He was smart, tough, and hardworking—it wasn't his fault if people wouldn't give him a chance. Ajay made a silent promise to himself—he would try even harder. Jai's dream of being a cricketer would succeed!

"I need to go," said Yasmin reluctantly. "We've got a special visitor coming to the factory from overseas. Mr. Gir, the manager, wants us all there."

Her words broke the spell in the room as they all realized the time. The drumming of the rain seemed to get louder.

"I should go too," said Vinod with a sigh. "It's the evening shift at the restaurant." He stopped, then looked at all of them and said quietly, "Thank you for celebrating my birthday."

"Of course we were going to celebrate. You are now one year older than you were yesterday, Vinod bhai!" said Ajay. Of course it wasn't quite true—none of the railway kids knew exactly when they were born. They just stole the birthdays of their favorite actors. Still, birthdays should be celebrated. Ajay looked around him happily. All his editorial team were there working and celebrating together: Yasmin, standing up with a nervous energy; Jai, his guard down for once, looking relaxed in the corner; Vinod, looking shy and overcome with emotion; Saif, slumped with his hands on his stomach, his expression one of sleepy satisfaction.

With their mixture of brawn, wit, and intelligence, how could they possibly fail in getting the story of the century? Then they would become recognized and rich, and be able to eat curry all day, and each have a luxury bed to sleep in—with feather duvets—instead of sleeping on the platforms, under newspapers, being lashed by the rain. Ajay rubbed his hands. The dream was so close he could almost feel the feathers tickle his nose and the warmth from the bedcovers. It would not be long now.

Chapter Seventeen

Pressed against the metal grille of the air vent, his body cramped and chilled, Ajay grimaced. How had he gotten himself into this mess?

It had all started so simply. After Vinod's party, he had followed Yasmin out of the platform room into the dark evening light. The wind, whistling like a restless ghost, was picking up, bringing with it sheets of rainwater that drenched them both.

"I should come with you to the factory—to see the overseas visitor," said Ajay, trying to shake off the rainwater.

Yasmin looked at him skeptically. "Why?"

"It is news!" beamed Ajay. Then, because it was Yasmin, his face fell and he confessed. "And I have no other news for the next edition of the paper. Of course, when our investigations into the slum clearance are complete, I will have enough news to fill all the newsstands in India! And America too," he added for good measure. "But for now . . ."

Yasmin didn't look impressed. "What story can there be at my factory? Buyer orders more T-shirts?"

Ajay felt his shoulders slump.

Yasmin looked at him, then sighed. "I'm going to wish I hadn't done this." She glared at him fiercely. "Okay—you can come. But stay hidden. If Mr. Gir finds you, I'm finished."

And that was why Ajay was squashed up, like a football

with all the air taken out of it, in a tiny vent. The sound of the rain hitting the metal roof boomed in his ears, and his bare arms stuck to the ice-cold aluminum sides. Through the rusty metal grille he could look down at the factory laid out below. In one corner, men were trying to keep awake as they stirred huge vats of foul-smelling blue dye. In another, women, including Mrs. Jodha, who he knew from the slum, were wiping their stained hands over dust-filled eyes as they printed designs. Yasmin was one of them, her head bent as she followed the flower patterns. Ajay found himself wanting to do everything he could to make her dreams come true. In his mind's eye, he saw the two of them at work on the biggest paper in the city: he as editor and she designing her own cartoons.

Suddenly, the huge metal doors scraped open and in came the factory manager, Mr. Gir, dressed in a three-piece suit. With him was a young man in jeans and loafers and a baseball cap turned backward on his head. Ajay tried to listen to the two men against the banging of the machinery. It was clear that he wasn't the only one struggling to hear anything. Mr. Gir yelled, "Stop!" Everyone did. At once. Then one of the boys, who must have been half-asleep, suddenly dropped the prongs he'd been using to turn the cloth in the liquid dye with a clang. Mr. Gir looked up, every line on his face showing fury, and waved his hand. The security guards came forward and took hold of the kid. Ajay tightened his grip on the metal grille as the boy was dragged out of the factory. Ajay bit his lip to stop the cry of protest.

The young man in the baseball cap shrugged, then spoke—his vowels long, his accent American. "So, Mr. G, you're going to show me what my boss's money is paying for?" Ajay frowned. Despite the jeans, it was obvious that it was the young man who had all the power here.

Mr. Gir nodded, almost helplessly. As he took the young man around the factory, Ajay wasn't sure who he felt more sorry for—the boy who had just been thrown out, or Mr. Gir himself. Eventually, Mr. Gir and the young man came to a stop by the wall in which Ajay's air vent was set. Ajay pressed his head to the side, hoping his shadow couldn't be seen on the opposite wall.

"Good job, Mr. G," said the young man, looking around. He turned back to Mr. Gir. "To the matter at hand: You will"— he gave a small smile that made Ajay's skin crawl—"confirm for my boss's lawyers that none of these workers is a child?"

"Of course, of course!" said Mr. Gir. "None of my workers are children."

Had Ajay misheard? What was Mr. Gir talking about? Half the workers were children! The young man had just seen that! Why was he asking such a silly question?

"Good. You'll just need to confirm that in writing. The document has been prepared. And now I have something else to discuss with you—in private."

"Let's go to my office," said Mr. Gir.

Ajay, watching them move toward the office at the end of the big warehouse, groaned. He would have to follow them. A fearless reporter like himself had no choice. He pushed himself along the air vent that ran along the top of the wall. The narrow passageway hurt, and there were only brief pools of light from the open metal grilles. He closed his eyes and wished he hadn't eaten quite as much bhiriyani.

At last he got to the corner, and turned, and found himself at another air vent. He could hear Mr. Gir and the young man speaking. He peeked through the metal grille covering the hole. The young man was sitting below him on a twisting chair. Every so often he would spin around. Didn't he have any manners? Ajay was affronted. Mr. Gir was unpleasant, but he was twice as old as the young man and was being forced to stand uncomfortably to the side.

"Get it sorted, Mr. G," said the young man lazily. "Those prices come down—or we find ourselves another producer."

Mr. Gir flushed. "But—you must understand—we are already charging as little as we can. And this building—it's the one we are using under your contract. But there are cracks in the walls and pillars—the surveyor says that they are dangerous and that we must get them looked at. Otherwise the whole building could collapse and kill everyone inside!"

"Mr. G, you're disappointing me. The company's customers have gotten used to buying cheap clothes."

Ajay blinked. He strained his ears, trying to hear more.

"As for this building—my company has a contract with the builder, one of the most powerful men in Mumbai. We get certain advantages with you using it." The man continued, "It is completely safe. You can rely on me. After all, have you ever heard me lie to you?" His lazy voice stopped, almost taunting Mr. Gir with the silence that came after.

Ajay felt his stomach turn as Mr. Gir shook his head mutely.

"Good. I expect the prices you are quoting for the production of the T-shirts to drop—tonight. Now sign this piece of paper to confirm that no children work here. I want to show it to some people who have been asking too many questions. The fact that there are kids here is something that only the two of us need to know."

Ajay gasped as he realized that he had his story: "Buyer of T-shirts (with terrible taste in baseball caps) lies about children working at the factory." The metal vent echoed the sound of Ajay's intake of breath . . . loudly. The young man twisted his chair around, but Ajay ducked back inside the vent quickly before he could be seen, his heart hammering in his chest.

Chapter Eighteen

Mumbai was drowning. The skies were black and rain thundered down, causing the ground to become slick and treacherous. The monsoon season had started in earnest now.

Ajay sat on the platform, shivering. He had been up all night in his room writing the story about the factory where Yasmin worked. He looked at the paper that he was holding between ink-splattered fingers and reread what he had written. The story was brief. Not his usual style at all. He had just written about the factory and the man with the baseball cap and the children working in the dark and cold, and the brand of T-shirts—and the condition of the factory building. That was it. He had wanted to add extra flourishes, but somehow they didn't seem to fit the story. Ajay took a deep breath and stood up, looking around. The clock showed it was five in the morning, but there was no light, just rain hitting the station roof like shards of scrap metal and the wind screeching through the windows like a braking train.

He went down to the engine room. The door creaked as he opened it and switched on the light. He had not been there as early as this before. It looked eerie—the broken engines and giant mechanical parts lying cold and glinting in the sparkle of the single bulb that fizzed with yellow light. He padded softly through the room, scrunching his nose at the smell of oil, avoiding the odd rusty metal screws that lay littered on the floor where a plastic bag had spilled open.

He heard Saif before he saw him. A grunting snore that ended in a soft buffet of air. Ajay saw a mass covered by old issues of *The Mumbai Sun* that fluttered up and down in time to the snore.

"Wake up!"

The snores just got louder.

"Saif."

Louder still.

"Brother Saif!"

There was a pause. And then the snores resumed—even louder.

Ajay whipped away the newspapers and saw Saif curled up, asleep, holding a spanner and an oil-flecked rag in his arms. He prodded the mass. "Saif!" No reply.

There was nothing for it. Ajay took a samosa that he had been saving for just such an occasion and whispered in Saif's ear, "I have breakfast . . ."

One of Saif's eyes opened. Then the other. He looked at Ajay, frowned, then looked at the samosa. He shot up.

"Give me that!"

Ajay gave it to him and Saif started eating, talking between hurried mouthfuls.

"What are you doing waking me up so early? I am an apprentice engineer! I need sleep to recharge my batteries, keep my senses alert, my brain sparking. I need to be in tip-top condition. If I make a mistake—all of Mumbai will come to a standstill!" Having finished the samosa, he glared at Ajay.

"I am sorry, Saif, but this cannot wait. I have a new story for *The Mumbai Sun*. It must go out today."

Saif glared at him harder still, and then crossed his arms for good measure. "You are telling me you have woken me up to print a story?"

Ajay nodded, then held out his last samosa as an offering. "Please, Saif—it's important."

———————————

The type was set, the paint was rolled, the paper was fed in. Saif was rolling the presses. Sheet after pink sheet was printed. At the end of the print run, Ajay picked up one of the sheets. The paint was still wet. The words gleamed by the lamplight that Saif had turned on.

"Are you really going to distribute this, Ajay bhaiya?" said Saif, sounding worried. He leaned precariously against the red button that was the station alarm, capable of waking up everyone in the station and within a mile. "Yasmin may not wish you to."

"Of course she will, Saif!" said Ajay, beaming. "It is to be a surprise. Everything will change for her and everyone in the factory. After this edition, they will work in better conditions and be warm and happy. Just wait and see!"

By seven o'clock, despite the rain, he had managed to sell every copy of *The Mumbai Sun*. He had done it alone—not asking any of the others to help him. All his readers would know about the factory. It was only a matter of time before Yasmin found out too.

Chapter Nineteen

Ajay sat on the platform. He hadn't seen Yasmin for days—since the last edition of the paper.

The rain was lashing down in lines so thick and so dark that it was as if black snakes were hissing down. The trains had stopped and stood silent, deep in dark water. The railway kids wading back from work had brought reports of the sea-walls that protected the city being battered. There was no one else on the platform with him. Everyone was huddling inside, trying to keep warm and dry. She wasn't coming. He should go in too. He was just about to turn inside when he heard Yasmin's voice.

"Ajay!"

He turned around instantly. She was drenched, but barely seemed conscious of the fact. Her eyes were flaming; her hands were tight in fists. She was shaking.

"Yasmin. You are cold! You must come inside into the warmth." He reached out a hand. She shoved it away from her and he suddenly realized that she wasn't shaking from cold but from anger.

"How could you, Ajay? How could you write the story?"

He didn't understand why she was so angry. "You mean about the factory? It was news. I thought you would be happy."

"News?" Her voice rose. "You mean you did this just because

of the paper? You destroyed everything just because you wanted to print the story?"

What did she mean, "destroyed"? He tried to explain. "No. No. Listen to me—people need to know about the factory. They need to know that . . ."

"You've not heard, have you?" Yasmin said.

Ajay stopped. "Heard what?"

She laughed, her voice catching, out of control. "Once you printed your stupid paper, other journalists came."

Ajay brightened for a moment. "But that's wonderful! They read the story. Then everything is going to change?"

Her eyes became hot with fury. "Oh yes, they read the story. Then the foreigners said that they had not known the conditions, but now that they do, they will stop buying from the factory. It can't survive without that contract. We've all lost our jobs!"

Ajay felt the blood drain from his face.

"Did you hear, Ajay? The factory's closed. There's no work for any of us," Yasmin said.

"That's not possible," Ajay breathed.

She didn't reply. Just stood there—still and accusing. He felt as if he had been punched. Those jobs were all the people who worked there had. Without them, they would starve. He had seen people starving—eating tree bark to stave off the gnawing ache. How could he be responsible for that?

"There must be something that we can do . . ."

"Haven't you done enough?" said Yasmin, her voice like bitter gourd.

"Please—let me make it right."

"You can't," she said flatly. "I'm going to the factory with Mrs. Jodha on behalf of our teams to speak with Mr. Gir. I'm going to ask if we can say to the foreigners that we don't care; that we're happy about working in the factory. No matter how bad the conditions are, it is better to work than not work."

"Let me come with you to explain," he begged, touching her arm. "Please, Yasmin."

She shook him off. "Stay away from me. I don't want to see you again."

She turned and walked away from him, back into the rain and the wind and the darkness. He stood alone on the platform and buried his head in his hands.

Chapter Twenty

It was Niresh who found him. The old station attendant had come out to the platform to check that the sign that was swinging wildly in the storm wind was still secure. He had taken a deep breath when he saw Ajay with his head buried in his hands, then taken him to the glass-paneled station office at the back of the platform, where there was a stove and where he made some chai with condensed milk.

"Drink," Niresh said gently.

Ajay could barely make out the word. Niresh handed him the mug. "Drink," Niresh said again. Ajay felt the warmth of the mug and drank automatically.

"Can you tell me what's happened?"

When Ajay didn't say anything, he asked again. "Is it about the story? About the factory?"

"They all lost their jobs," Ajay said at last.

"Ajay . . ." Niresh began.

"And it's all my fault," Ajay continued. "It's all my fault."

Niresh got up. Ajay closed his eyes. He could hear Niresh go to the shelves and rustle around.

"Ajay."

He looked up. Niresh was flicking through an old book with faded red covers and a half-broken spine. After a moment, he found what he was looking for. "Read this."

Ajay slowly took the book from him and looked at the page where Niresh was pointing: *"Fi-at ju-stitia ruat cælum,"* he said aloud, halting at the strange words.

Niresh nodded. "Let justice be done though the heavens fall."

Ajay didn't understand. Niresh must have gauged the expression on his face. "It's Latin." Ajay felt even more confused.

"I've not always wanted to be a station attendant," said Niresh gently. "When I was young, I wanted to be a teacher. Of course, the gods decided otherwise, but I realized that in my breaks I could learn things. Someone left this Latin textbook on the platform." He sighed again. "The quote is right. Once you knew about the story, you had no choice. It was the right thing to do to publish it—justice had to be done no matter what the consequences."

"Even if it means that Yasmin will never speak to me again?" Ajay said bitterly.

Niresh looked grave. He was silent for a moment, but then spoke quietly. "Even then."

"No!" Ajay cried, standing up. "You're wrong!"

Niresh looked as if he was about to say something when the door flung open. Vinod was standing there. The words burst from him. "Come quickly! Yasmin's factory . . . it's collapsing."

"What do you mean?"

"The roof—the walls—they're all collapsing under the weight of the water!" Vinod was shouting now, distress in every line of his face.

"Is anyone inside?" Niresh's voice was urgent.

Ajay broke in. "Yasmin. She went there to speak to Mr. Gir. She's there." And he felt terror overwhelm him.

Chapter Twenty-One

"I'll ring for help," said Niresh, but Ajay and Vinod were already out of the station. They ran through the slum that was slip-sliding in churning mud and black water. At some points they were wading. At others they were swimming. Ajay choked as a wave of dirty water went over his head—the street was now a river of slime. Vinod reached down, pulling him out by the hand.

They rounded the corner to the factory, which was on slightly higher ground, and found the way blocked. People from the slum had gathered and were standing in the road, paralyzed. Ajay pushed his way through, wanting to scream. He looked up as the massive concrete building groaned. A crack like a thunderbolt ripped through its wall. The corner of the factory crumbled in a sudden explosion of gray boulders and dust that covered them like ash.

Everything was veiled in gray and white.

Ajay couldn't breathe. He lurched forward. He had to find her.

"Stop, Ajay! It's too dangerous." Vinod caught his arm, but Ajay shook him off violently and kept running. Bits of rubble were still falling from the walls of the factory. It had only been built last year. How could it be collapsing? He put his arms up as a loose shard of rock tumbled and fell, hitting the ground in front of him.

"Yasmin!" he cried. But his voice was lost in the sound of crashing concrete, thundering rain, and shrieking wind.

"Yasmin!" he cried again.

No answer.

He looked up. The broken walls of the factory had jagged edges, and gaps, like eye sockets, where the windows had been. Somewhere in there Yasmin was lying injured—or worse, dead. No—he would not let himself think that. She was in there . . . alive.

Think! he told himself. He had to think. He had to save her.

The corner of the factory had collapsed, but Mr. Gir's office was on the other side. Ajay took a deep breath and ran into what was left of the warehouse.

Inside it was pitch-black. The electricity must have sparked out. There was a creaking above him, and a sudden rush and clatter as roof tiles smashed down. Rain and light sloshed in through the gaps. Ajay clambered over squares of concrete. At one point his hands were slick with sticky red liquid. Blood? Ajay shrank back in horror—then realized that it must be the vats of dye that had spilled, leaching their liquid all over the floor and walls.

Another crash of falling tiles.

He could see a figure coming toward him.

"Yasmin!" he cried out, scrambling to get to her. His heart beat painfully in his chest.

But the figure stumbling against him wasn't Yasmin. It was elderly Mrs. Jodha—her hair half-tugged out of her bun, her face covered in dust and cuts.

He grabbed her. "Mrs. Jodha!"

"Outside. I must get outside," she murmured.

"Mrs. Jodha. I need to find Yasmin."

She looked at him blankly.

"Yasmin. Where's Yasmin?"

She shook her head, unable to speak. Tears were falling down her face. "Gone."

He refused to believe her. "Tell me where she is."

She shook her head. "She went to speak to Mr. Gir. The roof collapsed. She couldn't have survived."

Ajay's hands dropped to his sides.

Mrs. Jodha gathered herself. "Save yourself, Ajay!" Then she left, stumbling out of the factory.

Ajay pressed his hands against his head.

No. Mrs. Jodha was wrong. Yasmin was alive. She had to be.

If Yasmin had gone to speak to Mr. Gir, it would be at his office.

He hurtled his way in that direction, his legs cut by stray pieces of concrete. But the door to the office was blocked by a heap of rubble.

"Yasmin! Mr. Gir!" he shouted against the stones.

There was no sound.

"Yasmin!"

Silence.

"Yasmin . . ."

Nothing.

Ajay's knees gave way. Emptiness opened up inside him as

he fell to the ground. Mrs. Jodha was right. Yasmin couldn't have survived. It would just be her body inside with her bones broken under piles of concrete. He shook uncontrollably, knuckling his eyes.

And then, suddenly, through the rubble, he heard the sound of banging.

"Yasmin?" he whispered.

His eyes opened.

The banging continued. Faint, but definite. As if someone was hitting the wall.

Hope flared like the light of a match. It was all he needed.

"Yasmin!" he shouted joyfully.

She was in there! She had to be in there.

And he had to get her out.

He jumped up. Water was pooling around his legs. Soon what was left of the factory would be flooded. He had to remove the rubble, but how? Yasmin needed him—he would not panic! He examined the rubble, the way he'd seen Saif examine machinery. Most of the stones were piled on top of one another—but there was one blocking the door arch that was not supporting the rest. It was like the Jenga game left on the train that they had given to Vinod for his birthday! All he had to do was remove the stone, without toppling the others around it, and everyone would be saved.

"I'm coming, Yasmin!" he shouted, then sped to find one of the trolleys used to lift the boxes of T-shirts. There was one, fallen on its side. He righted it and dragged it with all his strength to the blocked doorway.

Another creak. This time from the central pillar holding up what remained of the factory.

Ajay stuck his tongue out to the left, as he always did when concentrating. He maneuvered the trolley so the base fit underneath the stone, then carefully used the handles to lift it up.

One misstep and all the stones would topple on one another, trapping Yasmin forever.

Ajay took a deep breath and pulled backward on the trolley.

The stone slid out like a slice of chocolate burfi, leaving the rest above it like a pyramid. He almost wept with relief.

"Yasmin!" he shouted through the gap the stone had left.

"Ajay! Help us."

Her voice was so faint, he could barely catch it.

He went down on all fours and crawled in through the gap.

Chapter Twenty-Two

It took a moment for his eyes to adjust. Water was everywhere and more than half of the roof had collapsed. He saw her before she called out to him.

"Ajay!"

She was on the floor, her left leg pinned to the ground by the table that had collapsed on it. In her hand was the curtain rail that she had been using to hit the rubble and make the sound that he had heard.

He ran and flung his arms around her. "Yasmin, you are safe!" Then he added, "And I have come to rescue you."

"The table, Ajay!" Her voice was weak.

He lifted it up, like he'd seen weightlifters do. His arms felt like noodles. The table slipped from his hands with a crash.

But it had been long enough for Yasmin to snatch her leg out.

"Are you okay?" he cried.

Yasmin was gingerly touching her leg. She nodded. "It's bruised, but I can move it, I think." She stood up and cried out, stumbling.

Ajay caught her. "It's okay, I am here to support you." His heart felt warm.

She leaned on him and closed her eyes for a moment. But when she opened them again, terror sparked in them like flashes of lightning. "Ajay! Mr. Gir! He was here. I was speaking to him when the roof fell in."

Ajay looked around. At first he couldn't see the factory manager anywhere. He opened his mouth to tell Yasmin.

Then he saw the body. It was lying on the other side of the table, partially crushed under broken tiles.

Mr. Gir was a big man, and he lay on his side with tiles covering his large frame like scales. Ajay went over to him on tiptoe. Mr. Gir lay there, with a huge gash on his head. His eyes were open, glassily staring into nothing. His skin was drawn tight against his skull, his lips already edged with blue. Ajay had seen people die before, of course, but it was usually through the slow ravages of hunger, or through illness. Not like this. Ajay clenched his fists—tears welled up, burning his eyes. It didn't matter that Mr. Gir could be a bully; he didn't deserve to die like this.

Behind him, Yasmin spoke urgently. "Ajay? Is he okay? Ajay . . ."

How could he tell her? He dashed the tears away and turned slowly to face her. For the first time in his life he had no words.

She didn't need them. She must have seen the truth in his face. She let out a single strangled cry.

Ajay caught her and held her tightly. How could he make this better? How could he make any of this better?

There was an earsplitting sound from outside the room. Ajay turned around. The pillar! It must be beginning to crack. If they didn't go now they would be trapped forever.

He turned back to Yasmin. "We have to get out of here. Now."

Yasmin looked at him in shock. "We can't leave him."

He grabbed her wrists. "He's dead, Yasmin—we have to get out."

As if hearing his words, the pillar creaked again—only now the sound rippled over them as if the very fabric of the building was tearing apart.

Yasmin shuddered. "The factory should never have collapsed like this." She gathered herself. "We have to find out who built it and make them pay. Promise me, Ajay." Her eyes fixed on his. "Promise me that we'll make them pay."

"I promise!" he replied, clasping her hand so that she knew he would keep his word, no matter what happened.

There was a moment of stillness . . . then the rest of the roof started to collapse.

"Now!" cried Ajay.

He pulled her with him as he dived down and back through the hole in the rubble.

Chapter Twenty-Three

In the main section of the factory, stones and tiles were raining down like lightning bolts, smashing on the ground and splitting into smithereens.

"It's no use!" said Yasmin, soaked to the skin with the black water. "We can't get out."

Ajay refused to give up, even though every path was blocked by debris.

"We will find a way, Yasmin!"

But *which* way to turn? Which way to get out?

Suddenly, a horn blasted in front of them.

Was he imagining it?

Then they heard Saif's voice calling from the distance. "Brother Ajay! This way! Saif, the apprentice engineer, has come to rescue you!"

Ajay and Yasmin both turned toward the sound of the horn and the voice, and twin headlights appeared, coming toward them. Ajay gave a hoot of triumph. Saif was driving the small forklift truck that the factory workers used to move the dyes from the warehouse, with Vinod and Jai holding on to the sides. The truck was weaving erratically, and Ajay suddenly wondered if Saif had actually ever driven before. It careered to a halt in front of them. Vinod and Jai, the tallest of the group, jumped off and ran toward Ajay and Yasmin, lifting the smaller stones out of the way. The truck spun a couple of times, but then the fork-lift charged into action and cleared a path to them.

Jai grabbed Yasmin; Vinod grabbed Ajay. They pulled them into the side of the truck, squashing Ajay and Yasmin into the passenger seat next to Saif while the two of them held on to the edges of the frame. Saif waved at them. "Welcome to my truck! Of course, it is not my truck—it is the truck of the factory. But as apprentice engineer I am able to—"

"Get on with it, Saif!" growled the voice of Jai from above them as he hit the roof, his body pressed against the side of the tiny truck.

Saif frowned at being so rudely interrupted, but then pulled down on a yellow lever with a flashing bulb on the end. The truck spun around. Ajay saw stars circling his eyes.

"Oops! Sorry—wrong one!" said Saif as yelps could be heard from Jai and Vinod, holding on to the carriage for their lives. "Ah, is it this one? Or perhaps—"

"Saif!" cried Ajay warningly.

"You cannot hurry this. It is a fine piece of mechanical engineering. Ah—this should be correct!" Saif pulled down a red lever. The truck stopped spinning and rolled backward at speed, crashing through the broken stones, out of the central doorway, and squelching to a stop in the churning mud outside.

The monsoon rains were still coming down.

As if at a signal, Vinod, Jai, Yasmin, and Saif jumped out of the stopped truck. Ajay was the last to clamber out and join the group. Arm in arm, the five stood and stared at the shaking factory in front of them.

They had saved themselves only just in time.

A second later, the factory caved in. With a roar and crash of concrete it crumpled in on itself, letting out a jet of fragments of stone and tile that whirled into the air.

It had been utterly destroyed.

And it had taken Mr. Gir's life with it.

Ajay clenched his fists. "We're going to find out who was responsible for building this factory," he said, his eyes fixed on the cloud of dust.

"And we're going to make them pay," finished Yasmin.

Chapter Twenty-Four

Ajay stood in the Kamala Nehru Park looking at the Old Woman's Shoe. It was a huge sculpture, and kids were scampering around, through, and up it, while their mothers, wearing sparkling bangles, and fathers, wearing shirts and ties, laughed and looked on. He came here when he felt so much inside that he thought he would explode. He only had fragments of memories of his mother that he hoarded like rubies—the most precious of which was coming here and holding tightly to her hand just before she had abandoned him on the railway. He remembered the storm of emotion in her eyes as she had knelt beside him, starlike flowers in her hair, smelling of jasmine and dust.

Normally he would stay here, allowing himself to think about her and feel close to her for just a few hours. He would watch the other mothers caressing their children's hair, or giving them a samosa to eat, or even getting annoyed by the tugs on their saris, and feel his heart beat, but today he walked quickly away.

His head was churning. He thought about his mother, and then about Mr. Gir, who had been there but was now dead. Even though he had seen the body, Ajay still couldn't really believe it. Did people who disappeared always leave a part of the universe missing, like a hole in a piece of fabric?

Ajay bit his lip. He and *The Mumbai Sun* had to get justice for Mr. Gir. They had to! Not just because he had promised Yasmin, but because maybe—just maybe—it would help a little to stitch together a bit of the hole that had been left when Mr. Gir had died.

There was a crackle of thunder in the sky. A few raindrops started to fall. They were fat, and cold, and refreshing. Ajay lifted his head and opened his mouth to catch some of them.

He would have to leave soon, but before he did he ran to the Ashoka pillar with its statue of the four lions, the state emblem of India, and took a deep breath. It towered above him. The lions looked stern but benevolent. He would be brave like them.

Chapter Twenty-Five

Ajay, balanced on the tree branch he had found at the last protest, felt himself beginning to explode. His anger had started popping like mustard seeds in oil when Mrs. Shania, the politician in charge of the area who'd talked about the slum move, had started to speak. Her red nails had gleamed as they picked up the microphone. She had looked at the crowd and smiled her trademark smile—one that showed all her teeth. Then she had begun. "We are, of course, *very* sad about the collapse of the factory. It seems that the manager, Mr. Gir, a *terrible* man by all accounts, had let the building fall to ruin, so that when the rains came it simply collapsed. Still, he himself was the one to pay the ultimate price—proving that the gods always ensure that we get what we deserve." Here she rolled her eyes upward for effect, as if she was looking for a sign from heaven.

Ajay took a grape and aimed it at her head. Bull's-eye! She looked up, horrified, as if she wasn't sure whether it was a raindrop or a bird dropping. Ajay raised his hand. She saw him, and her expression stilled. She turned away.

"But Mr. Gir wasn't to blame!" Ajay cried out. He had to catch her attention.

"You know nothing about it, child!" snapped Mrs. Shania, whirling back to face him. Then she reassembled her face back to a smile. "You are too innocent to understand."

The gathered crowd of businessmen and journalists, some who he knew, others who must have been foreign, murmured in agreement. The people from the slum and those who used to work at the factory had been kept away from the conference, behind barriers. It was only because Ajay was so small that he had managed to sneak in and find his place on the tree branch again.

"Mr. Gir wasn't evil. He wasn't nice, but he wasn't evil," said Ajay firmly. The crowd of rich people would hear the truth. "The builder of the factory was a crook but Mr. Gir was forced to use him. Mr. Gir warned an American buyer in a baseball cap that the building was unsafe, but the buyer didn't care."

Mrs. Shania's eyes narrowed, like someone who had spied a rat in their kitchen and was wondering what way of dealing with it would cause the least mess. "You are a boy who has no idea what he is talking about."

Ajay's anger expanded like a bubble. He puffed out his chest. "I am the editor of *The Mumbai Sun*! I have the facts. I was there. What I say is true!"

A man stepped forward to whisper in Mrs. Shania's ear, then stepped back.

She looked up. Then she spoke again—but this time it was loud enough for the back of the crowd to hear. "*The Mumbai Sun?*" She shook her head and shrugged, facing the crowd. "It is a sad time indeed when we get our news from illiterate street kids! Talk about fake news. What next? Will we get headline updates from animals?"

There was a ripple of laughter in the crowd.

Ajay flushed, but from anger rather than embarrassment. "We only print the truth!"

Mrs. Shania shrugged. An exquisite shrug that suggested the difficulty of dealing with children who would not be silenced. "As I was saying, the factory and its terrible manager have perished. The building company has also gone into liquidation, so it no longer exists—therefore nothing more can be done about it." Here she shot a look at Ajay. He shot her one back, furious. "We must now look forward," she said, turning to smile at the crowd. "Firstly, we are lucky that the collapse of the factory was a freak occurrence. Secondly, we continue to welcome foreign investment, so we are lucky that we have builders who can be trusted to do the right thing with our most innovative and expensive of projects. And thirdly and finally, we are lucky and incredibly grateful that we have Mr. Z to create new buildings for those who currently live in the slum—a slum that is due to be renovated in just seven days' time!"

There was a raucous cheer. Ajay frowned. All the journalists were clapping their hands. Only Mr. Gupta, editor of *The City Paper*, was standing apart, looking pensive. Ajay could hear two foreign journalists, under the tree branches, speaking. "What can you expect? A corrupt factory manager. Mr. Gir was his name, wasn't it? This really is the problem with developing countries—they just don't know how to deal with local corruption. And then international companies get caught up in the mess."

All the anger that had been bubbling inside Ajay rose to the surface like lava. What were they saying? That only places like India had buildings that collapsed? He remembered how much he had cried when he had seen photos in the papers of the tower block in London that had gone up in flames. The fire had killed many of those inside. Had they forgotten already? Corruption was a problem everywhere! So was the death of the innocent.

Ajay swung off the tree and landed in front of the two journalists. They jumped back in shock, covered in a shower of leaves that fell from the tree. They looked as if they were about to laugh, then stopped as Ajay gave them a look of utter contempt. He watched them wither under his stare, then turned away. He didn't have time to waste on them. He had a job to do. He had to find the builder who had deliberately built an unsafe factory and bring him, and anyone else involved, to justice. This was his job—his watch. No matter what it took, he would make sure that *The Mumbai Sun* told the truth.

Chapter Twenty-Six

They stood at the door to the crumbled building in Colaba. It was made of custard-yellow sandstone and the windows were boarded up with wooden planks nailed to the frames with metal spikes. The black wrought-iron balconies above them were almost hidden under twisting lime leaves that glinted in the bright sun.

"Are you sure this is the place?" said Saif, scratching his head.

"It's the registered address of the company," said Ajay confidently, knocking at the door with a loud rap. No answer. "Yasmin remembered the name of the builders from the sign on the factory wall when it was being built: 'Factory and Idyllic Strong Houses and Yard Builders.'"

"The FISHY builders," interrupted Saif.

"Yes," said Ajay impatiently. "The FISHY builders. Niresh looked them up. This was the address listed for the director in charge of the company. It must be right." He felt very official, holding the spiral notebook with the address in his hand. He even had his mother's pen tucked behind his ear. He knocked again.

No answer. His confidence deflating a little, Ajay stretched on tiptoe and peeked in through the letter box. All he could see was darkness.

"I am only an apprentice engineer," said Saif with dignity. "What would I know about it? But do people in charge of building companies generally live in closed-up buildings?"

Ajay heard the turning of latches from inside, like the inside of a safe, and the scratching and scraping of a bolt being pushed back. He felt a tremor of fear, then stood back and stretched himself to his full height, squaring his shoulders. The director of the FISHY builders was likely to be a thug—a brutish man willing to destroy the lives of thousands; a bully. Ajay put a terrifying frown on his face. He was ready for him.

The door swung open. Saif took a step behind Ajay. Ajay held his breath and gripped his notebook and pen, ready to write.

Out stepped a frail old woman, balancing herself on a stick, her eyes almost milky. Ajay put down his hands and stared.

"Yes?" she said hesitantly. Her voice fluted up in the air, as thin as reeds.

Ajay twisted his head to look at Saif, who looked back at him and shrugged. Ajay interpreted the shrug—*You decided to come here. I am just an apprentice engineer. This is your mess*—and sighed.

"Is Mr. Somchand Omar Shikand in, please?" he said as gently as he could.

The old lady looked confused.

"Yes. But he is eating. What do you want with him?"

"It's a business matter," said Ajay quietly. *Mr. S.O.S. has a lot to answer for*, he thought, his insides bubbling again. This elderly woman had clearly been hoodwinked into thinking Mr. S.O.S. was a good man. Ajay didn't want to be responsible for the sadness welling up in the old woman's eyes when she realized that her son—or nephew, or whatever—was a crook.

The old woman nodded uncertainly, then called out behind her. "Somchand! Somchand! Can you come here?"

Ajay held his breath, hearing the sound of chairs being scraped back and the clatter of cutlery from inside. Footsteps could be heard running toward the door. Ajay clenched his jaw.

"Somchand," said the old woman.

"Yes? Dadi?"

Ajay rubbed his eyes and looked down. Next to the old woman was a toddler—a boy with big eyes, bigger eyelashes, and ketchup smeared over his mouth.

Ajay turned back to the old woman, who was looking at him expectantly, tenderly holding the little boy's hand in her own delicate, blue-veined one.

"I am sorry," said Ajay, flustered. "I'm looking for Mr. Somchand Omar Shikand. The older one," he added, in case it was unclear.

"This is Somchand. And there is no older one. Somchand's parents died years ago. It is just me and him," said the old woman protectively. "Now what do you want with my grandson?"

Ajay tried to rally his thoughts. "Is he a director?"

The old woman looked at him as if seriously doubting his sanity. "No. What do you mean a director?"

"The man in charge." Ajay tried to explain himself better. "I mean, according to the register he is the man in charge of a building company called the FISHY builders. But of course it can't be him. I mean, he must only be two years old." Ajay stopped, flustered, realizing that he was babbling.

"I'm three," said the boy indignantly, squashing a fry into his mouth.

The old woman looked at Ajay as if dealing with someone from Mars.

"I'm sorry," said Ajay. "My mistake." Disappointment and confusion churned inside him. He swallowed hard and broke eye contact. The old woman hesitated.

"Why did you want to find this particular building company? I am sure there are many builders who can do the work you need instead," she said gently.

He shook his head. "No, I need to find the FISHY builders. You see, they're the ones who built the factory. The one that collapsed."

The old woman flinched. "Did—did anyone die?"

"The factory manager. Mr. Gir."

"I'm sorry," she said, "I'm so sorry."

Then she withdrew back into the house with her grandson and shut the door behind her. Ajay could hear the bolts and latches being scraped back into place. A sharp wind sent a scatter of lime leaves around him from above. Ajay hung his head. It was a dead end. There was no chance of getting justice now. Whoever had built the factory so badly that it had collapsed was going to get away with it.

Chapter Twenty-Seven

Ajay and Saif trudged back down the street. Ajay's head was bowed. Saif seemed quite cheerful now that the danger of facing up to a thug was past.

"Those fries looked good," he said. "And that ketchup. Personally, I prefer salt and chili and lemon, and perhaps some spice." He licked his lips. "But of course ketchup would do if you were really hungry."

Even the thought of the fries didn't cheer Ajay up. What could they do now? They hadn't been able to find out who was behind the FISHY builders. There was no news for the paper to print, and no news that he could give Yasmin. Ever since Mr. Gir's death she had looked at him with eyes filled with a mix of anguish and anger. All he had wanted was to wipe that look away. And they'd reached a dead end.

"Sir! Young sir!"

Ajay turned at the voice and the *slap-slap* sound of sandals behind him. It was the old woman, balancing herself on her cane and waving papers in her hand. He and Saif ran to her as quickly as they could.

"I am glad to have caught you," she said breathlessly. "I have these for you." She pushed some papers into Ajay's hand hurriedly, as if she wanted to do it at once before she could change her mind. He looked at them, confused.

"What are they?"

"Envelopes and letters sent to me with checks every month. Checks that could be cashed to provide us with money."

"For what?"

She closed her eyes for a moment. Then she opened them again. At that moment, the sunrays happened to glow on her, lighting up her amber skin and white hair. Her voice when she spoke was still thin, but firm. "When my husband and son died at a building site, a man came to see me. He said that some important people had known my husband, and so they would look after me and my grandson."

Ajay was scribbling as fast as he could in his notebook. "There was a condition?"

She nodded. "That I move to this house with my grandson."

"That's all?" said Ajay, swallowing his disappointment.

"That's all," the old woman confirmed.

"I don't understand," piped up Saif, looking from one to another. "Why have you come to tell us this?"

"Because there was another condition. That we never tell anyone about the arrangement."

Ajay smiled, suddenly understanding.

"I don't get it," said Saif, still sounding confused.

"Because secret money and silence are a bad combination, brother Saif!" said Ajay. "I learned about it in a film with two journalists who met someone called . . ." He racked his brains for a moment. "Well, I can't quite remember—I think it was someone called Big Mouth—and he tells them 'Follow the money!'

That's what you're asking us to do, aren't you? To follow the money?"

The old woman looked for a moment as if she was questioning her own sanity in trusting Ajay with the papers. "I don't know what film you are talking about, but it's too much of a coincidence: We're being paid in secret to stay here and at the same time this address and my grandson's name are being put on documents linking us to the factory builders. Builders who you say are the same as those responsible for someone's death. Yes, I want to know where the money is coming from."

"Why?" asked Saif.

"What do you mean, 'why'?" said Ajay. "Isn't it obvious?"

"No, it isn't," said Saif. "Not at all. It's obvious why *you* want to know—you want to know because of Mr. Gir and Yasmin and because you can put the story in the paper. But it's not obvious for her—or her grandson. You publish the reason why she's getting the money, and nothing will happen to you. But she and her grandson could lose everything—their home, and money, and, well, *everything*," he concluded lamely.

Ajay's eyes widened. He had never thought about it like that. How brave people had to be if they were going to do the right thing. Suddenly, he felt his insides crumple up with guilt: Was it even all right to ask someone to risk so much? He looked up at the old woman and knew that she read the wordless question in his eyes.

The old woman was quiet for a moment. "You're right—we might lose everything. But I want to be able to look myself and my grandson in the eye." She put her hand on Ajay's shoulder, and for a moment he wondered what it would be like not to be an orphan, to have a mother or grandmother like this to hug him when he felt lost. "Be smart, and honest, young man. We're counting on you."

Ajay felt tears brewing inside him. He could only nod.

She turned away and shuffled back to the custard-yellow house.

Ajay felt realization dawn. Not all heroes were famous. Not all wore medals or sporting trophies or capes. Some heroes were just ordinary people, doing an extraordinary thing—holding on to their integrity no matter what the cost.

"Be smart," she had told him. "And honest."

He would be both. For her, and for himself, and for those hurt by the collapse of the factory.

He took the fountain pen from behind his ear where he always kept it and stared at the black casing and the gold tip on the lid. For a moment he wondered whether his mother was still alive, and whether she ever thought about him.

He put the pen back behind his ear.

He was doing this for her too.

Chapter Twenty-Eight

He found Yasmin at Marine Drive, the sea promenade that ran along the edge of the city. He clambered down it and tumbled into the sand. The beach was thronged with tourists and residents alike. Acrobats were spinning on their heads, vendors were selling postcards, and kids were playing games of catch and chase. He could see her in the distance, framed against the setting sun, which was turning everything the color of burnt sugar and saffron.

He ran to her, excited to tell her the news from that afternoon. In his hands he carried the envelopes with the letters given to him by the old woman, and boxes of warm bhel puri that Vinod had packed for them both at the station. He stopped short as he came close to her. She looked up at him, and he almost stepped away at the ferocious look of concentration in her eyes. In her hands she held a stick. On the sand were lines that had been drawn, lines that were half scuffed out, lines that were half formed but still showed the sharp features of politicians' faces that Ajay recognized.

"What is all of that?" he blurted.

Yasmin continued looking at the sand and Ajay wondered if she'd even heard the question. Just as he opened his mouth again, she answered grimly. "Practice."

"For what?"

She looked at him as if seeing him for the first time. "For the cartoons."

He was puzzled. "But they're great! You don't need to practice. They're brilliant. You are like . . . like . . ." He scrunched up his face, trying to think of a famous artist. "You are like Mickey Mouse!" he said triumphantly.

"I am like Mickey Mouse?"

Her voice was cold.

"No," said Ajay, blushing. "The people that created him."

"Walt Disney—and Ub Iwerks."

"Yes, them." He squirmed. Why, ever since his and Yasmin's falling-out, did all the words tangle when she was around?

She sighed. "But I want to be like me. I can see the cartoons in my head—I can see them clearly. But when I try to draw them, they're nothing like that. I can't capture them. That's why I haven't drawn any for *The Mumbai Sun*."

"But these are beautiful!" he said again.

"I don't want them just to be beautiful," she said tiredly. "I want them to be powerful. I want to change the world with them. Just like you want to with the words in your paper."

He didn't know what to say, so he held out the box of bhel puri. She hesitated, then took it from him. Soon they were ravenously devouring the mix of puffed rice, fried dough, cubed boiled potatoes, garlic, and tamarind paste that Vinod had prepared. Ajay felt his eyes water as he crunched through the sweet and tangy flavors. Vinod was a genius! He glanced up at Yasmin, who smiled at him as if her earlier cares were forgotten, although he knew that wasn't true. Behind her, the lights of the seawall curved like a double strand of yellow diamonds—the Queen's Necklace. In the background a radio was playing songs from the latest Bollywood blockbuster.

"So, what are the envelopes about?" asked Yasmin after they had demolished the food and carefully washed the containers in the salty seawater so that they could be reused.

"Hmm?" Ajay was broken out of his reverie.

· "The envelopes."

He took them out of his pocket, where he had placed them for safekeeping while they ate.

"I don't know—only that they're a lead from the grand-mother." Briefly he filled her in on what had happened that afternoon.

Yasmin picked up some coral-pink shells to use as paper-weights as they laid the envelopes and letters in front of them.

"This is useless," said Ajay after a while, sitting back on his haunches with a frown. "Just a bunch of letters from a lawyer saying 'Dear Mrs. and Mr. Shikand, we enclose a check as per our client's monthly agreement with you.' What use is that?"

"Not so fast." Yasmin was looking at them intently. She picked up one of the thickly embossed papers. It had a golden sheen in the light. "Look—you're right. They all say the same thing—except for this one: 'Dear Block Surveyors, we enclose a check as per our client's monthly agreement with you.' They must have made a mistake and mixed up two letters."

"How does that help us?" said Ajay, his head beginning to hurt. He took the letter from her and read it. "Oh . . . I see."

Yasmin smiled, and Ajay felt that flush in his cheeks again.

She hadn't looked so happy for a long time. "If the lawyers were paying the lady and her grandson for something dodgy, they might be doing the same with the surveyors. After all, surveyors check that buildings are safe. Why would you pay them something in a monthly agreement—not just a one-off payment for a particular job?"

"But how do we know that it's related to the factory?"

Yasmin's smile became an outright grin; her eyes danced. "Because I remember the name: 'Block Surveyors.' They came to the factory a month ago. Mr. Gir asked them to come to do the report for him on whether the factory building was safe or not."

Ajay scratched his head and remembered back to the conversation between Mr. Gir and the man in the baseball cap. What were the exact words that Mr. Gir had said? He took out the spiral notebook that he now carried with him everywhere, flicking through the pages of hastily written scrawl: . . . *there are cracks in the walls and pillars—the surveyor says that they are dangerous, and that we must get them looked at.*

He felt excitement flowing from him like lit fireworks. "The surveyor knew that the building was dangerous," he said to Yasmin. "All we need to do is get them to show us the report and tell us who's paying them. Then we can write an article about it and everyone will know the truth!"

"Careful, Ajay," Yasmin warned, putting her hand on his arm to draw his attention. "It might not be as easy as that."

"Of course it will!" said Ajay, his excitement replaced with a feeling of confusion. He felt conscious of her hand on his arm.

"They'll do the right thing. Remember the old woman and the grandson!"

"Not everyone is like them . . ." Her voice trailed away.

She looked as though she was about to say something more, but then she moved her hand away and looked back out at the beach and the cartoons she had drawn on the sand. Ajay looked at them too. The sea, with its dark muscles of water, was pulling in and out. They waited and watched together as, one by one, each of the cartoons was gradually washed away.

Ajay suddenly found the words he wanted to say to her about them. "It's okay, Yasmin. The cartoons will get better. You'll get better. Just keep drawing. That's the important thing. Not to give up."

Yasmin nodded, blinking back tears.

Then her voice grew firm. "I'll keep drawing, but first let's go and find the surveyor."

Chapter Twenty-Nine

In the end, they had to wait until the next morning for the surveyors' building to open. It was rammed between a jeweler's selling chains of intricately worked gold, and a cooking shop selling polished copper pans. As they waited outside, Ajay and Yasmin spent considerable time making funny faces at the pans, giggling at the distorted reflections that shone back at them.

Suddenly, the blinds in the surveyors' shop windows and glass door rolled open, revealing the sign BLOCK SURVEYORS. Ajay and Yasmin turned to each other and entered the shop together.

The bell on top of the door rang on their arrival. Ajay took a deep breath. The surveyors' shop smelled of pencil sharpenings and sawdust, and its walls were lined with pictures of beautiful-looking buildings. Inside there was a stand-up desk with a huge piece of paper marked up with pencil drawings; next to it was another desk with a computer and phone. A man with big wistful eyes looked at them, startled, from behind it.

"Yes, can I help you?"

Ajay decided to come straight to the point. "I am here because of the factory."

The surveyor's face became pale. He didn't even ask which factory. His thin hands held the desk, trembling.

Ajay decided to take a gamble. "You wrote a report saying that the factory was unsafe—I want a copy of it. And"—he decided he might as well go for the jackpot—"I want to know who is paying you money to keep quiet about it."

The surveyor's fingers tightened on the desk. "I knew this day would come," he whispered. Then he stood up. Just as he did so, another man jangled in, with an oily mustache, slicked-back hair, and gold rings on his fingers. Ajay wouldn't have been surprised if he had them on his toes too.

"Who are you?" the oily man demanded.

"I am the editor of *The Mumbai Sun*. This is the illustrator of *The Mumbai Sun*," he said, motioning to Yasmin. She inclined her head.

"What do you want?"

"They want to know about the factory," whispered the pale-faced surveyor.

"They do, do they?" The eyes of the man with the oily mustache narrowed like a cat that has just spied a mouse.

"Yes," said Ajay, undeterred. "I want a copy of the report and I want to know who is paying you to keep it secret."

The man with the oily mustache looked at them and then started to laugh, showing all his teeth. "You want? You want?" Abruptly, he stopped laughing and came closer to Ajay, bending down to stare at him, until all Ajay could see were his red-flecked eyes. "Who are *you* to want anything?"

"I am the editor of the—"

"*The Mumbai Sun*? What is that? What circulation does it have? You are a paper that people use for toilet paper! How dare you come here and want anything!" He was shouting so hard that spittle was flying from his mouth.

"Stop that!" shouted Yasmin.

He stood upright. "You don't know who you are dealing with. Get out, both of you. Or I'll call the police."

"Call them!" said Ajay, infuriated. "And I'll tell them about the bribe."

The man sucked in his breath, then grabbed Yasmin's arm tightly enough to make her yelp.

Ajay ran at him but was blocked by the pale-faced surveyor, who had desperately gotten between them. "Please, Amrij sahib, they are just children. Leave them to me—I'll get rid of them."

At that moment, Yasmin kicked the oily man in the shins. He fell, nursing his bruised leg. "Why, you—"

Ajay pushed past, ready to tackle the man to the ground, but Yasmin pulled him back.

"Let's get out of here, Ajay," said Yasmin, glaring at the oily-faced man. "Before anything else happens. This bully isn't going to tell us anything."

Ajay was shaking as he tried to keep his anger in check. All he wanted to do was attack the man who had hurt Yasmin.

"Please, Ajay," said Yasmin again. "Deal with him later—through the paper."

Ajay glared at the man, then turned with Yasmin to the door. The pale-faced surveyor opened it. As Ajay and Yasmin stormed out, he followed them. "Tell them—the people from the factory—that I'm sorry," he whispered.

Ajay looked at him with contempt.

"Please—you don't know who you are dealing with. My

job, my career, my income—I have to stay quiet. I have to protect everything I have built."

Ajay let all the rage that had been bubbling under the surface ever since the collapse of the factory burst through. "All you 'have' to do is tell the truth, and you won't do that. You're nothing but a coward."

The last thing he saw, as the door shut between them, was the pale-faced surveyor behind the glass, looking as if someone had punched him in the stomach.

Chapter Thirty

Ajay sat on the station platform watching the gleaming trains rumble past. Normally watching trains lifted his mood, but today was different. Without the report from the surveyor there was no way of finding out who was in charge of the FISHY builders—and therefore the person responsible for Mr. Gir's death. *The Mumbai Sun* motto was "Truth alone triumphs," but instead of uncovering the truth, all they had uncovered was dead ends.

They hadn't even been able to find out anything more about the slum, even though the excavators were coming in four days' time.

What if the oily-faced man at the surveyors' was right? What if *The Mumbai Sun* was only good for toilet paper?

Ajay sighed. When he was younger, he would spend every moment of his spare time sitting on the platform, among the trains and the passengers and the porters and the drivers and the food sellers, hoping against hope that his mother would be on one of the trains arriving at the station, coming back for him. As he'd grown up, he had imagined himself going on the train as a reporter to far-flung places with magical names like Jaipur—the Pink City; Jodhpur—the Blue City; Bhopal— the City of Lakes. And recently his dream had expanded as he had imagined one day traveling with Saif, Vinod, Jai, and

Yasmin across India, to investigate stories for *The Mumbai Sun*.

But what was the point of dreaming when every dream came to nothing?

Ajay shook himself out of his own thoughts.

Even if he had to give up on his own dream, he still had to fight for justice for Mr. Gir and keep his promise to Yasmin.

And if *The Mumbai Sun* did not have power, maybe it was time to go to someone who did.

Chapter Thirty-One

Ajay had waited near the fig tree all morning. The sun had scorched the back of his neck. He knew he had not gotten the time wrong: even without watches, growing up in the shadow of the railway clock, all the railway kids could tell the time to the minute. ("Like superheroes!" Ajay had boasted just that morning—Yasmin had raised a sardonic eyebrow, while Jai had just drawled that he couldn't wait to see people running to see a movie franchise called The Punctuals.) Then at last Ajay saw Mr. Raz walking past Mr. Sandhu's stall in a (spotless) white suit.

"Mr. Raz!" Ajay waved.

"Ajay." Mr. Raz walked over, looking as elegant as ever. His green eyes were merry. "Mr. Sandhu gave me your note and told me that it was with regard to a very important matter. Shall we sit down so you can tell me all about it?"

Ajay nodded and waited for Mr. Raz, who, after signaling for a glass of lemon water from a vendor and signing a couple of autographs and doing a few selfies for shy well-wishers before politely moving them on, sat down with him on the small bench encircling the fig tree.

"Now tell me what you and *The Mumbai Sun* need." Mr. Raz smiled, giving a glass from the vendor to Ajay, who gulped the lemon water down thankfully. "After all, I do see you and the newspaper as something of a personal investment."

Ajay took out coins from his pocket and held them out. "This is what I owe you for the paper from Mr. Sandhu."

Mr. Raz shook his head. "There's no need for this. I was only joking."

"A journalist has to be independent at all times," Ajay said, insisting.

Mr. Raz hesitated, but at last, very serious, took the money, part of Ajay's share of earnings from *The Mumbai Sun*. "Thank you. And now bring me up to speed."

Ajay put his thoughts in order before blurting them out. "The textile factory collapsed because the building was faulty. The builders were called the FISHY builders, but we want to know who actually was in charge of them."

"Have you looked at the company's records?"

"We don't think the records are right," said Ajay carefully. He trusted Mr. Raz, but he would speak about Mr. S.O.S. and Mr. S.O.S.'s grandmother only in an article and not before. A journalist must protect his sources!

"I see," said Mr. Raz. "And you want me to help find out the truth of who was in charge of them?"

Ajay nodded. *The Mumbai Sun* had reached a dead end. It needed help, and Mr. Raz was the most powerful person he knew. Actually, if he faced facts, Mr. Raz was the *only* powerful person he knew.

Mr. Raz nodded thoughtfully. "Very well. I'll try—as a special favor, you understand. It will be good to have *The Mumbai Sun* owe me one!" he joked, but then turned serious. "But, Ajay, the likelihood is that the builders and their owners have long disappeared. You must understand that sometimes in this world we cannot make everything right."

Ajay nodded, even though he didn't really believe it. People had to *try*.

Mr. Raz stood up, looking at the fig tree that threw dappled shadows over his white suit. "I will come back to you tomorrow with what I find. In the meantime, I must hurry back home to make some calls to London regarding a tree grove." He put his hand on Ajay's shoulder, his green eyes kind. "I know that the collapse of the factory has been a tragedy for the community. But things are getting better for people, Ajay. In just three days from now I will be cutting a ribbon for the destruction of a slum. I have no doubt that people living there will feel it as a loss to start with, but sometimes great projects, like the planting of trees, just take a bit of vision to see through to the end result. Not all people have the foresight required to see that vision come to life. But you, like me, have it in you. Hold on to that."

"Destruction of a slum?" asked Ajay, looking up with interest. "Do you know Mr. Z, then?"

Mr. Raz shook his head. "No one knows him personally. But I believe that people in the slum deserve a better life, so when Mrs. Shania asked me to cut the ribbon, I wanted to be part of it." He looked at his watch. "And now I really must go. Remember, Ajay, if you ever need anything, you only need to ask."

Ajay watched him go, feeling hopeful for justice for Mr. Gir thanks to Mr. Raz's promise to help, but deflated inside. He'd had such dreams for *The Mumbai Sun,* but the oily man at the surveyors' had been right. It didn't have enough power. To have more power it needed to sell more papers, and to sell more papers it needed . . . Ajay straightened, his eyes snapping with sudden glee. He knew exactly what it needed!

Chapter Thirty-Two

Ajay and Jai were sitting on the bench outside the Headmaster's office at the Churchill School, the most exclusive school in Mumbai. The secretary and the Headmaster were conferring inside. Ajay had brought Jai up to speed with Mr. Raz, what had happened with the surveyor and how Ajay had blamed the surveyor and called him a coward.

"I think you were too harsh," said Jai. "It sounds like the surveyor was trying to apologize."

Ajay couldn't believe what he was hearing. "He *was* a coward," he repeated firmly. "Evil people only survive because of people like him. People who don't say anything. The police won't believe anything without proof, so now our only chance is Mr. Raz—and even he isn't sure he will be able to find anything. Why are you sticking up for the surveyor?"

"People can't always be defined by the worst thing they have done," Jai said quietly, staring at his cricket bat.

Ajay was about to reply when the heavy oak-paneled door swung open and the secretary walked out of the room in a huff. The Headmaster, a tall, proud-looking man with graying hair and wearing a long black cloak, came to the door, looking at them wearily.

"Come in."

Jai and Ajay entered, feeling overawed. The window was

diamond-paneled glass, and curved outward, creating a little bay. In front of it was a large desk with papers, a green lamp, and a coffee flask. The rich smell of coffee mixed with the smell of books and polish, and Ajay breathed it in greedily.

"Please sit."

Feeling nervous, Ajay clambered onto a green leather-bound seat that was so tall his legs dangled off the edge. He looked around. The walls were lined with books: books about law, Latin, and linguistics; books to do with science and geography; books to do with history—not just of India, but of the Caribbean and of Africa. Ajay suddenly felt very aware of all the knowledge he lacked. What was he doing here? A boy who had never even been to school, here, in a school that had produced some of India's most powerful men.

"Coffee?"

Jai shook his head, but Ajay nodded, still too nervous to speak.

The Headmaster brought out two gold-embossed mugs displaying the school's coat of arms, poured in the coffee, and added cream. He handed one mug to Ajay.

"Cookies?"

Ajay nodded again, as did Jai. Food should never be turned down.

The Headmaster offered them a box of ginger cookies and Ajay took a handful and hastily stuffed them in his mouth. They were crumbly, dark, and delicious. He felt instantly better and wondered for a moment if the Headmaster knew he was nervous and was giving him time to settle down. He took another handful.

"Now then," said the Headmaster, sitting back in his seat. "What can I do for you?"

"Weroioihoieo," said Ajay through the second mouthful.

The Headmaster looked at him blankly. "Excuse me?"

Ajay drank some coffee to wash down the rest of the cookies and cleared his throat. "We want a match."

"I don't understand," said the Headmaster slowly. "My secretary said that she received a call from *The Mumbai Sun* about doing a piece on the history of the school."

"She tried to stop us coming in!" said Ajay indignantly. "Even after I'd made that call and the appointment with her and everything."

The Headmaster coughed a little. "Yes, well—I think she was a bit surprised. You see, I expect she had thought it would be someone older."

Ajay frowned.

The Headmaster shook his head. "Ah, well. Never mind. What is it that you want?"

"I told you—a cricket match—with your best team, and ours. Jai's the captain." Ajay pointed at Jai, who squirmed in embarrassment.

The Headmaster took another sip of his coffee. "I'm sorry," he said finally. "That just won't be possible. Our sports teams only compete with other private schools. The governors will not like it if they play against anyone else."

"Please . . ."

The Headmaster shook his head. "I'm sorry."

Ajay felt defeated. The feeling he'd had when coming into

the office came back. The feeling of not being good enough. Perhaps if he had gone to a school like this, he would have the knowledge and the skill with words to make the Headmaster understand. The cricket match had to take place! Without it, people would stop reading *The Mumbai Sun*, and the oily man who'd shouted at them at the surveyors' would be right—the newspaper would be powerless.

He looked around in desperation for something to help him. On the walls were paintings of previous head teachers. He looked back at the bookshelves and saw, in among the heavy tomes, a copy of the history of Tipu Sultan. Ajay looked back at the man sitting in front of him and suddenly felt a bond of connection with him.

"It is better to live like a lion for a day than like a jackal for a hundred years," Ajay quoted.

The Headmaster looked startled.

"It's true," said Ajay. "You need to give us a chance."

"I wonder . . ." The Headmaster stood up suddenly and faced the window.

Ajay and Jai held their breaths.

After what felt like hours, the Headmaster turned around. "This school is called Churchill School," he said. "Sir Winston Churchill helped to win the war against the Nazis—with the contribution of Asian, African, and Caribbean service members who sacrificed their lives in fighting for freedom when they themselves were not free. But there was another side to him too—his policies, to take just one example, led to the death of at least three million people in India during the 1943 Bengal famine. He continued with those policies even when officials pointed out to him that those deaths were needless."

Ajay wondered why he was giving them a history lesson.

The Headmaster continued as if Ajay had asked the question out loud. "Our students have a strong belief in themselves—but going to a school like this does not in itself make you better or more intelligent. It just gives you confidence in the rightness of your decisions—a confidence that can be wonderful but can also be entirely misplaced." He opened the window and a sharp gust of air blew in, scattering the papers on his desk. He opened a drawer and took out a ball made up of elastic bands.

"Jai—is that your name?"

Jai nodded, bewildered.

"Can you see that bird feeder, in the tree at the other end of the field?" He pointed out the window.

Ajay and Jai both looked. Ajay could only just about see the tree, never mind the feeder, but Jai nodded.

"If you can hit it, you get your match."

"But that's impossible," shouted Ajay, jumping up from his seat.

"Shut up, Ajay!" said Jai with quiet ferocity. He stood up and took the ball of rubber bands and bounced it experimentally on his cricket bat a couple of times.

"Ready?" said the Headmaster.

Jai didn't answer. He just bounced the ball again a couple of times, and then suddenly smashed it with his bat. The ball flew through the air, shedding bands as it went like sparks from a lightning bolt, toward the tree. Ajay couldn't see it as it hit the bird feeder, but he could see birds that were squawking furiously and flying up into the sky. The Headmaster punched the air with his fist, then looked embarrassed. "Well done. You did it. I've never seen anything like that shot before."

"We have our match?" Jai's voice was low, filled with a burning intensity. It was only now that Ajay realized how much the chance to play against the best junior team in Mumbai meant to him. He held his breath.

The Headmaster nodded. "You have your match."

Ajay and Jai leaped up and high-fived each other, cheering. The Headmaster smiled.

Just then, there was a knock on the door.

"Come in," called the Headmaster, looking up.

A boy came in with a sheet of paper and seeing Ajay and Jai almost did a double take.

"Bharat, good timing. We have two guests," said the Headmaster.

Bharat put the sheet of paper on a tray marked REGISTERS, his eyes sliding coldly over them. Ajay felt him taking in their ragged clothes and appearance, and the cricket bat in Jai's hands.

"You will be playing them and their team in a cricket match."

"But, sir!" Bharat said quickly.

"That will be all—inform the others."

"But—"

"That will be all." The Headmaster's tone was very mild, but there was a finality to it.

"Very well, sir." Bharat turned to go out, but not before giving Ajay a long look.

"Perhaps this has happened not a moment too soon," the Headmaster murmured, watching Bharat as he left.

"But what about the governors?" asked Ajay. "Could they overturn your decision?"

"Mr. Raz can inform me of the governors' views, but that is all. For the time being at least, I have control over this. The match will go ahead."

"Mr. Raz is a governor? The environmentalist?" Ajay asked.

The Headmaster nodded. "He's the head governor and will be at the match. He always attends. Do you know him?"

"He's helped me," Ajay said, nodding. He rubbed his hands in excitement. He had gotten what he wanted. The match to end all matches. He would write about it in the next edition of the paper.

Powerless? Not likely. News of the cricket match meant that *The Mumbai Sun* was just about to become one of the most popular papers in the city.

Chapter Thirty-Three

Ajay and Jai whooshed down the streets back to the railway, laughing and jumping and whooping with glee. Ajay felt like a rocket on fire. Jai looked transformed, with hope and wonder sparkling in his butter-colored eyes. They burst into the engine room of the railway station, their words tumbling over one another in their excitement.

"You'll never guess—"

"Churchill School!"

"They've agreed. They've actually agreed!"

"A cricket match in two weeks."

"And *The Mumbai Sun* has exclusive coverage!"

It was Ajay who stopped short first, realizing that something was wrong. Vinod was slumped against the wall, his glasses in one of his hands, his eyes red from crying. Saif was crouched next to him, trying to comfort him with a plateful of sticky dates.

"What's wrong? What's the matter?"

Vinod looked up and Ajay saw that his face was streaked with dried tears, with a dark bruise on the left side of his face.

"He was sacked," said Saif.

"What?" said Ajay. "Why?"

"Mahesh found out I was writing the recipes for *The Mumbai Sun*, that's why," said Vinod. Ajay had never heard him, the most good-natured of them all, sound so bitter. "He said I worked for him, and no one else."

"I don't understand," said Ajay.

"What's there to understand?" Vinod straightened so that he was standing and facing Ajay. "This morning I had a job and now I don't." He laughed suddenly, but the laughter was mocking. "Why am I worried about cooking? I don't even have enough money to eat anymore."

Jai stepped forward, his face still beaming from the news of the cricket match. "Don't worry, Vinod. You can come with me—I'll teach you how to beg. It's not so bad really."

"I'm a cook, not a beggar!" Vinod snapped.

Jai recoiled as if he had been hit. All light extinguished from his face. The softness in his expression was replaced by hard angles. His eyes turned dark like rusted coins and his mouth twisted in a cynical sneer. "Of course you're not," he said quietly. "Begging is just for people like me. How did I forget that?"

Ajay stepped in. "Jai, he didn't mean it! He is just upset."

Jai turned toward him and Ajay felt he was looking at a stranger.

"Who are you to talk?" Jai spoke with a lethal softness.

"I'm the editor of—" Ajay started to say automatically, before he could stop himself.

There was a moment of silence as Jai's eyes blazed. "Yes. The editor. That's all you care about—and all you do."

"But Jai . . ."

"That and make empty promises. I don't need them. I was

happy before—before all of this, before all of you. I didn't need anyone."

"Brother Jai, they weren't empty promises. We have the cricket match. You will play against Churchill School, just like you always wanted."

"You think I don't know why you did that?"

"I did it for you! And for the . . ." Ajay's voice trailed off.

"Exactly. You did it for the paper. Like you do everything. You want to be a journalist. That's all you care about—the paper and Yasmin. The rest of us"—he pointed at Saif and Vinod—"we're just tools; things you manipulate."

"No, that's not true," Ajay protested.

Jai shook his head. "I'm tired of being used." Grief suddenly flashed in his eyes as he threw the cricket bat to the ground.

"Jai!" Ajay cried out, but Jai had already turned and run toward the slum, his dark figure lost to the evening shadows. He didn't once look back.

Chapter Thirty-Four

There was silence. Vinod slumped back to his haunches. Saif couldn't meet his eyes. Ajay looked from one to another.

"Jai's wrong! I don't use people," he said, then his voice fell into a whisper. "Do I?"

For a moment they didn't answer him.

He thought back to when he had gotten Saif to help him move the printing press, Jai to stand with his cricket bat at the station, and Vinod to write recipes. He had always thought he had been doing it for them all, and for the paper, and to get justice for Mr. Gir and Yasmin. But what if Jai was right and he had just been using them? After all, they'd all had their own jobs. It was only Ajay who really needed the paper. Everyone else had just been there because he had persuaded them in one form or another.

"I'm sorry," he said at last. He bit his lip, then tried to speak. "It's just that the paper is—well, it's . . ."

"We know, Ajay," said Vinod wearily. "We know that it's the only chance we have of getting justice for the factory and Mr. Gir, and maybe for us as well."

"Then why . . . ?"

Saif answered, his head bobbing up. "Because you forget who we are. You take us for granted." Saif began to warm to his theme. "It is always 'Saif this' and then 'Saif that.' You forget that I am an apprentice engineer. You haven't even noticed how much faster the printer works now. I spent two days changing the pistons."

Ajay looked at him wide-eyed, then turned to Vinod. "But you *wanted* to be a cook; Jai *wanted* to play cricket against the best team in Mumbai."

Vinod sighed. "You don't get it, Ajay. Yes, we wanted that. We even wanted you to help us. But because we're friends, not just because it's useful for the paper."

Ajay felt like he was going to be sick: It was like he had been looking through a telescope the wrong way round his entire life, and only now was seeing things in the right proportions.

He put his head in his hands.

"You're not the only one to blame here," said Vinod, his normally quiet voice rough with emotion. "I'm the one who started this today. I'm the one who lashed out at Jai because he was there."

"Yes, you are both to blame," said Saif, nodding wisely.

Ajay lifted his head. "I'm going to make this right. I'm going to find Jai."

"I am too," said Vinod. "But, Ajay—what if it's too late? What if he doesn't forgive us?" Ajay had never heard him in such pain.

"I mean, after what I said to him, why would he forgive us?" continued Vinod, and the bruises in his eyes were darker than those on his face.

"We have to try," said Ajay.

"It is all you can do," Saif added, with solemn intonation.

Ajay felt guilt tearing him up. He should have earned Jai's

and Saif's and Vinod's loyalty instead of demanding it. "We have to try," he repeated.

Vinod nodded. "Let's go, then. Now." He picked up the cricket bat that Jai had thrown on the ground. It was heavy, and Vinod was unaccustomed to its weight, but when Ajay offered to carry it, he shook his head. "No, I'll hold it. Come on, we need to go before it's too late."

Chapter Thirty-Five

By the time Ajay and Vinod got to the slum it was evening. The atmosphere was strange: On the surface it looked as if everything was going on as normal, with people cooking, eating, and arguing. But underneath, there was a crackle in the air—a sense of uncertainty; a sense of brooding fear. Posters about the slum clearance in just two days' time were glued on every fence and nailed on every tree, but with no information yet on where people would be moved to. Ajay had asked everywhere about the man with the golden tooth and his men, but there had been no leads. And with no new leads, there could be no story. In the distance, dark shadows of excavators could be seen looming above the slum, occasionally with a glitter of red lights flashing across them as if at some alien signal.

They could see Jai at his usual place, on the edge of the slum near the law courts, with a begging bowl—his proud frame hunched over. Lawyers with briefcases, cups of coffee, papers tied up with ribbons were all marching past, ignoring him. As Ajay and Vinod were running toward him, they saw four figures stopping by Jai and talking to him. Ajay felt himself stop for a moment, thanking the kindheartedness of strangers. But then they got closer and could hear what was being said.

"The great captain of the cricket team . . . here! Begging!"

"Too lazy to do any work?" said another boy.

The first boy knelt down so he was in Jai's face. Ajay wasn't sure what upset him more—seeing the boy being a bully, or seeing Jai, normally so proud and quick-tempered, just drop his head and not even flinch.

"It's the boy from Churchill School—Bharat," said Ajay, through gritted teeth to Vinod. He pushed up his imaginary sleeves, ready to jump in. "And his friends."

But Vinod wasn't listening. He was running up to the group, dropping the cricket bat at Jai's feet as he stepped protectively in front of him.

"What on earth!" One of the boys jumped back, but the other three formed a ring. Bharat was in the center. He was at least twice Vinod's body weight and looked like a boxer.

Vinod didn't seem to have noticed the fact that he was completely outmatched. He put up his spindly arms, ready to fight.

"Another street kid?" Bharat sneered.

Vinod was shaking. As Ajay came running up, he thought it was from fear, but then he realized it was something else. Normally Vinod was one of the gentlest of the railway kids, and one of the kindest. Yet looking at Vinod's eyes now, even Ajay was frightened. Vinod was shaking with fury—the anger in his eyes was like a raging bonfire that would consume everything if it was let loose.

Bharat laughed, although there was a touch of nervousness underneath it. "What are you? The captain's personal bodyguard?"

Vinod took one step forward. "No—his friend. And if you say one more thing, I'll . . ."

Ajay thought he'd better speak. "Look, wealthy sirs. It is better if you go. Normally I would keep you safe, but today . . ." Ajay pointed at Vinod and shrugged.

Bharat looked at Vinod and, seeing the rage in Vinod's eyes, stepped back almost imperceptibly. He tried to regain control. "Do you really think we're scared of a bunch of street kids?"

"Bharat bhai," said Ajay. "Look around. You are not on your home ground here. You forget—if it comes to a fight, we *railway kids* have nothing to lose."

Bharat was unpleasant but not an idiot. He looked around, saw other people from the slum coming over to watch, then signaled to his friends to go. "This is not over. At the cricket match, you'll be on *my* home ground."

Ajay nodded. "We're looking forward to it." Looking at Bharat and Jai, he suddenly had the flash of an idea. "In fact, we should make a bet on it!"

"You can't be serious!" said Bharat.

"I am!" said Ajay, with sudden glee. "If we lose, we will . . ." He thought for a second—what did people like Bharat want more than anything? "We will bow to you in front of everyone and acknowledge how much better you are than anyone else."

"You'd better count on it!"

Ajay frowned at the interruption. "But if *you* lose, you will apologize to Jai in front of everyone. You will admit that *he* is the better man."

"That's never going to happen."

"Then you will have no reason not to take the bet," said Ajay.

There was a pause as Bharat tested the double negatives to

make sure he knew what Ajay meant. Finally, he nodded. "Done. I can't wait to see you all groveling in front of me." He gave a signal and left with his friends.

Jai had stood up and was looking at Ajay and Vinod, his eyes shadowed.

Ajay hurried with what he was going to say: "Brother Jai. We're here to say we're sorry. You were right. We were wrong."

"Can you forgive us?" said Vinod—the anger was gone and he looked almost skeletal. "Can you forgive *me*?"

Jai looked at them for a long time.

Ajay held his breath. For a moment he thought he could see a friendliness returning in Jai's eyes.

Then it was as if Jai remembered everything that had gone before. The shutters went down. He turned away from them.

Ajay grabbed his arm. "We're sorry. You are our friend. We made a mistake. We're sorry."

Jai shook his head, as if he was trying to stop himself from listening. Ajay continued quickly, urgency in his voice. "Brother Jai. Let us make it up to you."

Jai looked at them warily.

"Please—you have to forgive us," said Vinod quietly.

Everything seemed to hang in the balance.

Jai looked from one to another. He looked at the bat and then at Vinod. The corner of his mouth lifted. He picked up the cricket bat from the ground.

Ajay breathed.

The shutters in Jai's eyes had opened. He was no longer a stranger. He had forgiven them.

Chapter Thirty-Six

Ajay and Saif were standing in front of a huge glass-and-steel building that reflected the light in a hundred different directions.

"Why are we here again?" Saif squeaked nervously.

Even Ajay was overawed. He shaded his eyes from the light that reflected down on them from all the glass, like a magnifying glass used to shrivel insects. "It is the plan!" he said, then turned to Saif with justifiable grievance. "In fact, it is *your* plan!"

It was true. At the celebratory dinner that Vinod and Ajay had thrown the previous night to mark the return of Jai, it had been Saif who had been looking at the letters the old lady had given them, with fingers sticky from the gulab jambu he was eating at the same time. He had looked at them with as much dignity as he could muster with a face smeared with golden syrup from the sweets. "We should go there!"

"Where?" Ajay had asked, completely perplexed. They had already been to the two people the letters had been addressed to: the builders and the surveyors. There was no one else. Even Mr. Raz had gotten nowhere. He had sent Ajay a beautiful hand-written note via Mr. Sandhu saying that although he had tried his best, he had to admit defeat and suggested that Ajay do the same, ending with the line: *Remember, there are other tree groves.*

Saif had snapped his fingers to get Ajay's attention.

"Not the people the letters were sent to, but the people *writing* the letters!" he'd said, pointing at the paper where the curved letterhead stood out in copperplate silver.

Ajay had blinked. "The law firm?"

"They'll have security. And cameras. And guards," warned Jai.

"It is a good idea though," said Ajay thoughtfully. *The Mumbai Sun* should not give up if there was any path left to investigate. Follow the money . . . and who had more money than a law firm? They would have information about the "client" paying them: the shadowy monster who was bribing the old woman and her grandson and the surveyors. Once they knew who the client was, they would know who was behind the destruction of the factory and the death of Mr. Gir.

"Leave it to me," Saif had answered. "I am an apprentice engineer. I know mechanics. What can go wrong?"

———————————

"Well?" said Ajay. "What's the plan?"

It was just the two of them. Yasmin was out looking for work, and Vinod and Jai, arm in arm, close friends once again, had gone out so that Vinod could learn how to beg. Ajay and Saif had taken the train to the center of the city—filled with banks, law and accountancy firms, and, arching over all of them, giant tech companies. The entire place smelled wealthy—of mint and crystal that seemed to rub Ajay's throat raw.

Saif looked up. "To get inside?"

Ajay nodded.

"Inside the building?"

Ajay nodded.

"Inside *that* building?"

Ajay could feel his impatience begin to grow. He nodded.

"Inside that building over there?"

"Yes," said Ajay shortly.

"Inside that building over there with the glass door and the . . ."

"Yes, Saif! How do we get inside that building over there with the glass door and the glass walls?"

Saif opened his mouth. Then closed it again. Then shook his head. "I don't know."

Ajay looked at him in consternation. "But I thought you had a plan!"

"I did. I've just forgotten it," said Saif hastily. "I am an apprentice engineer. I have many things to worry about and keep in my head. Many very important things. I cannot be expected to remember everything."

Ajay sighed. He looked up at the building and chewed his lip.

An hour later, he and Saif were walking into the marble reception area carrying a bucket of soapy water and an upside-down broom. Ajay occasionally tripped as he slipped across the marble floor. The white overalls that he and Saif were wearing—like the bucket and broom, borrowed from a friend of Vinod's—were too long, and the white caps were too big—so he kept having to lift a corner of his to see properly.

"This is not a good idea," said Saif.

"Have you got a better one?" asked Ajay.

Saif glared at him. "Not yet."

They had reached the reception area—a glossy desk with imported white flowers that looked like ivory dusted with gold, and gave a green silvery smell. Ajay drew in a long breath and sneezed loudly.

The receptionist gave a start above her desk.

Ajay sneezed again. She stood up and looked down at him, her eyebrow arched.

"Yes?" Her voice could have iced a refrigerator.

"We're here to clean the building."

"I'm sorry?"

She doesn't sound it, thought Ajay, warming to his character. "We're here to clean the building."

"Our building is already clean."

"That's because we did a very good job when we came last time!" said Ajay, trying to smile up at her, although his white cap was making it very difficult to see.

He could hear her voice, brittle, coming down from above. "I have heard nothing of this. Our contracted cleaners come in the evening." Her tone was imperious. "I need to have this checked. It is most irregular . . ."

Ajay improvised. "There is a reason for that," he said, trying to think of something.

Her eyes shone coldly. "And that would be?"

Ajay stood on tiptoe and spoke in a soft whisper.

The receptionist turned pale. All her superiority crumbled.

"Go!" Her voice was almost a shriek. "Here—take these." She rattled around in her drawer, bringing up two passes. "Now go!"

"Thank you," Ajay said courteously, taking the passes. He pulled on Saif's shoulder as the receptionist levered her chair up and up, until her feet were off the floor.

They got into the elevator. A shiny glass contraption in the middle of the building, it was full of gleaming buttons that Ajay wanted to press all at once. He chose the one that had the name of the woman who had signed off the letters. There was a soft hum and the elevator started going up.

"What did you tell her that changed her mind?" asked Saif in awe.

Ajay grinned. "I told her we were from pest control and that they had mice in the building."

Saif's brows knitted together. "One minute I'm an apprentice engineer, now I'm a mouse remover?" he grumbled. "Will it never stop? I am going to become an engineer. I have a reputation to uphold."

"Don't worry, brother Saif! It is only for a little while," Ajay soothed. "Just for as long as we—"

Ajay's words were cut off. The elevator had reached the floor of Mrs. Pain: managing partner of Pain and Proffiit Partners Law Firm, and the lawyer whose signature was curled in copperplate writing at the bottom of the letters.

Chapter Thirty-Seven

The door opened. Ajay and Saif fell out of the elevator, almost blinded by the blistering diamond light that fell on them through the glass walls.

"Now what?" said Saif, water from the bucket sloshing onto the floor. "I cannot carry this forever."

Ajay shielded his eyes from the light. "We go and find Mrs. Pain."

They walked through the corridor. All the offices had glass windows that scattered light in sharp fragments.

"How are we going to find her?" whispered Saif as they passed yet another person in a suit looking stressed.

"Jai said that the lawyers that walk past him always talk about the top people wanting 'the corner office,' so I guess we look there."

"But each corner is so far from the other one!" moaned Saif. "Why can't they all be next to each other?"

Ajay was saved from having to reply by seeing a young woman coming past them, her eyes looking red and raw as she carried some files.

"This way!" he said to Saif a second later, dragging him along the corridor in the direction the girl had come from.

"How do you know?"

"Someone horrible made that lady cry. It might be the same horrible person who's behind all of this."

They reached the office. On the door that was slightly ajar was a sign scratched in gold embossed writing.

MANAGING PARTNER: MRS. PAIN.

"Bingo!" cried Saif.

"Shhh," said Ajay, wrapping his hand around Saif's mouth and dragging him back. The corner office was angled so that there was the door on one side and a frosted glass panel on the other that prevented them from looking inside. Outside the office was another empty desk—that of Mrs. Pain's assistant, guessed Ajay.

"Quick, Saif!" He pulled on Saif's arm and they crept past the door and crouched to the side of the desk outside.

It wasn't a moment too soon. A telephone rang from inside Mrs. Pain's office and they heard it being picked up. Mrs. Pain's voice came through the door, low and musical.

"There will be no more loose ends. You can trust me. The only thing linking you and the collapse of the factory is the report, and I have just locked that in my personal safe."

A pause.

She spoke again quickly. "Do not worry, Mr. Z. I will deal with them."

There was lethal promise in her words. There was a clicking sound as the phone was put down, and then a moment of silence.

Ajay and Saif looked at each other in horror. Mr. Z, the Bollygarch that no one had ever seen, was the person to blame for Mr. Gir's death? Ajay clenched his fist, trying to keep his anger in check as it blazed. Mr. Z wasn't just in charge of the factory— he was in charge of demolishing the slums! They had to stop him—and that meant that no matter what, they needed that file.

Along the corridor came the sound of footsteps, and someone approached the desk. Ajay and Saif shrank as low as they could behind it.

The glass door to Mrs. Pain's office opened properly with a scraping sound. "Lata."

"Yes, Mrs. Pain." Lata's voice was young and carried in it the trace of tears held back.

"Is the photocopying done?"

"Yes, Mrs. Pain."

"That's good. And every page is perfectly straight? To the millimeter?"

"Yes, Mrs. Pain."

"Our clients demand the very best and it would be such a shame to find yourself, a junior with no connections, on the streets without a reference—particularly with your mother in the hospital."

"Yes, Mrs. Pain. I promise it won't happen again."

"I know it won't." There was a poisonous pause. "I am going for a champagne lunch. I will be back in two hours. I expect all the documents ready to sign and on my desk."

"Yes, Mrs. Pain."

They heard footsteps moving away, followed by the sound of Lata collapsing into a chair and taking deep breaths.

Ajay popped his head up. The junior lawyer—Lata—sitting on the chair was the same young woman that they had seen earlier. Her eyes were still red. She started when she saw him and Saif.

"Who are you?"

"We're the cleaners," said Ajay, offering her a tissue from the box on her desk. "We're here to clean the office."

She took the tissue, her face flushed. "You must have made a mistake—Mrs. Pain doesn't allow *anyone* in there."

Ajay showed her his pass that gave him and Saif security clearance. "This is a special reason." Then he added succinctly, "Mice."

"But . . ."

"You don't want Mrs. Pain to find one in her office when she comes back, do you?"

Lata trembled, and Ajay hated himself for using her fear against her. She shook her head, then stood up and opened the door. As he and Saif walked in, Ajay turned to her to try to mend things. "You know, she should be more afraid of you than you are of her—*you've* done nothing wrong." Before she could register anything strange about his words, he waved the pass at her again. "Now we'll close the door to make sure the mouse doesn't escape. It will take us about an hour and a half to clean everything and find it." She nodded blankly as he closed the door between them.

Chapter Thirty-Eight

Ajay, trying to hone his journalistic skills of observation, noticed three things about the office straight away. The first was the gray carpet, which looked so velvety he wanted to take his shoes off and run across it. The second was the giant glass desk at one side of the office, on which was a computer with a blank screen and a phone. Ajay shook his head in sorrow at those people who always kept their desks neat and tidy and insisted others do the same. When Ajay had his own editorial office, it would always be gloriously untidy—the sign of real work being done! He gave a little sigh at the dream of his own office and then looked across from the desk and saw the third thing: a bonsai plant on the ledge running low down along the floor-to-ceiling window. Ajay hurried over to it excitedly—a Japanese tourist at the station had once left a book behind describing bonsai plants, and he'd always wanted to see a real one for himself. But as he approached the tiny tree, he recoiled in horror—the book had shown pictures of beauty: lovingly tended trees and greenery; miniatures that conveyed a whole landscape in a single plant. This tree looked tortured, as if Mrs. Pain had enjoyed prying each leaf apart.

He turned to Saif, but Saif was staring wide-eyed at his own discovery—looking as if all his birthday and Christmas presents had come at once—for there, set into the wall, was a cast-iron safe with a spoked lock on the front.

"Saif?"

No answer.

"Saif!" Ajay shook Saif's shoulder.

"Hmmmm?" said Saif, as if waking from a delicious dream.

Ajay clicked his fingers in front of him. "Saif! This is no time to lose yourself in your thoughts."

Saif noticed him then, and sighed. "You don't understand, Ajay. This is a first-class piece of mechanical engineering. This safe is a thing of wonder! It is a marvel of metalwork. It is—"

"Yes, yes," said Ajay impatiently. "But can you open it?"

Saif interlaced his fingers and flexed his hands. "Stand aside, Ajay! This is work that only an apprentice engineer can do."

Chapter Thirty-Nine

An hour later, Ajay had almost ground his teeth down to nubs with worry and impatience.

"Saif! Is it done yet?"

Saif looked at him with a pained expression from where he had his ear pressed to the metal door of the safe. "This is a complex piece of machinery. It—"

"I know, Saif! But we don't have much time."

Saif closed his eyes, counting slowly, turning the spokes on the door clockwise, then counterclockwise, then back again. "I am waiting for the right clicking sound," he informed Ajay. "I have three of the numbers, and now I am waiting for the last one. Now be quiet so that I can concentrate." He put his finger in the ear that wasn't pressed to the safe.

The door behind Ajay scraped suddenly and a low, musical voice spoke. "And what do we have here?"

Ajay whipped around. Standing there was a woman who could only be Mrs. Pain. Her white knit suit was threaded through with silver and glittered subtly in the midafternoon light. Her hair was curled in a sleek bob and she wore pearls on her ears and around her throat. *She's beautiful*, thought Ajay for a moment. Then she smiled, and he shuddered. None of her beauty or wealth hid her malignancy. It was like a shiny veneer stuck on a rotting tooth.

They had to get out of there.

"Saif . . . !" cried Ajay, trying to break the spell.

Saif's eyes were still closed, all his concentration on the safe. "Shhhh," he said, waving one hand in Ajay's general direction as a sign of dismissal. "You cannot interrupt. This is important work. I am just waiting for the right clicking sound . . ."

Mrs. Pain looked at both of them, then twisted her head to the side for a moment. "Lata?"

Lata's face emerged behind Mrs. Pain's. "Yes, Mrs. Pain?"

"What were you doing allowing these kids inside my office?" Mrs. Pain's voice was as soft as kheer.

From where she was standing, Lata looked at Ajay and Saif and back again, fear in her eyes. "They said that . . ." Lata whispered, unable to continue.

"We're here to deal with the mice," said Ajay, desperately trying to deflect the attention from Lata. "Lots and lots of mice," he repeated, hoping that Mrs. Pain would have the same terrified reaction as the receptionist. He should have known better.

"Mice?" Mrs. Pain's smile widened slowly. "Do you know what pet I have at home?"

Ajay shook his head, desperately searching his pockets with his hands for anything that he could use.

"A snake. A beautiful hooded cobra. I feed it mice every morning. You see, unfortunately, I think you're lying to me. If we had a problem with mice, I would have dealt with it myself."

Ajay gulped.

Lata had turned white behind Mrs. Pain. "I'll call the police."

Mrs. Pain shook her head. "No. Not the police. I want you to call one of my private security guards so that this can be quietly dealt with. This is a personal matter. And, Lata . . ."

"Yes, Mrs. Pain?"

"I'll be dealing with you later. Now go and call one of my guards, discreetly, just like the nice little junior you are."

Lata nodded quietly and disappeared from view. Mrs. Pain stepped inside, closing the door behind her, so it was just her and Ajay and Saif.

Ajay backed away until he was next to the window. They had to get out of there. "Saif!" he cried urgently.

"Stop interrupting, Ajay," said Saif, his eyes still closed. "This is meticulous work. Only the very best apprentice engineers can do it. I am the very best, but I can only work in optimal conditions of calm and quiet."

Mrs. Pain raised an eyebrow, then turned to Ajay. "So, you must be the street kid from *The Mumbai Sun*. I am so glad to make your acquaintance. You've been causing me no end of trouble." Her smile reached her eyes and she licked her teeth, as if relishing the thought of how she would pay them back for it.

Ajay rallied, despite the fear knotting his insides. How did she know him? "Let us go now, Mrs. Pain, and I'll give you a chance in the paper to explain yourself. Tell your side of the story."

"Explain *myself*?" Amusement glittered in her eyes. "I think you've got things rather the wrong way around. But, please—do go on. Why would I need to explain myself?"

Ajay needed to play for time. "Your client, Mr. Z, is a crook.

And so are you." Ajay started counting out the pieces of the puzzle on his fingers. "Firstly, you help him construct cheap buildings that are unsafe to work in. Secondly, you assist him in bribing surveyors to hide their reports, which would otherwise show everyone how dangerous the buildings are. And then—even knowing that people could die inside them—you both offer the cheap buildings to big international companies, who get people like Mr. Gir and Yasmin to work in them." Rage built inside him, burning away all his fear to ashes, and his hands closed into fists. "You're both evil. And *The Mumbai Sun* will bring you and Mr. Z to account."

There was a sudden cheer from the direction of the safe. Both Mrs. Pain and Ajay looked at Saif, who was oblivious to them both, rubbing his hands in glee. "What did I tell you? A supersafe. But I, Saif, opened the safe! In the way that only an apprentice engineer of my standing can." He opened the safe and pulled out a single file from inside. He turned around looking at it, disappointment in his face. "Ajay, this is not a great prize for all the time I have spent unlocking the supersafe." He looked up and saw Mrs. Pain.

"Hello?"

Then, suddenly recollecting where he was: "Who are you?"

"I am Mrs. Pain."

"Oh," said Saif, visibly crumbling.

"Oh, indeed. This is my office, that is my safe, and what you have in your hands is my file."

"I see," said Saif, hiding the file behind him guiltily. "Uh— Ajay?" he squeaked suddenly. "Do you have a plan?"

At that moment, several things happened at once.

The door opened and a beefy security guard with a truncheon lurched in.

"Catch them!" cried Mrs. Pain. "And get that file!"

The guard ran toward them. Ajay threw the bonsai plant—ceramic dish and all. It hit the guard, who looked momentarily stunned before collapsing on the floor, the plant on his head as if it had sprouted there.

"I will deal with this myself," said Mrs. Pain, rolling her eyes and stepping toward Saif and the file with the fallen guard's truncheon in her hand.

"I am an apprentice engineer!" Saif blubbered. "I am not made for violence."

"Well, that's a shame, isn't it?" whispered Mrs. Pain, her suit and pearls glimmering.

"Ajay?" Saif whimpered.

"Right here, brother Saif!" shouted Ajay from where he had climbed onto the table.

Mrs. Pain twisted her head around to see him, all shimmering elegance, when bam! Ajay threw the bucket of soapy water that he and Saif had carried into the building all over her. She screamed in uncontrolled fury.

"Why, you . . . !" All the musical notes in her voice were gone. She was wearing the bucket on her head and was sopping wet. Water and soapsuds were creating a pool of water on the floor around her. "Guard! Get up and get them!"

"This way, Saif! Run!" Ajay caught the broom they'd brought with them in one hand and pulled on Saif's arm with the other, dragging him through the door. He then turned and pushed the broom underneath the handle, locking Mrs. Pain and the security guard in. There was a crash against the door. It wouldn't hold them for long.

"You will pay for this!" screamed Mrs. Pain.

Ajay turned to Lata, who was half sitting, half standing by her desk. He took his cap off. "I'm sorry, Ms. Lata, for getting you in trouble."

Lata looked at him, then at the door that was beginning to crack from the banging inside, then back at him. Other guards, called by the noise, were running down the corridor toward them.

She took a deep breath, then pushed Ajay the other way. "Go! Quickly. There's an elevator that the cleaners—the *real* cleaners—use on the other side of the building."

"Why are you helping us?" said Ajay, shocked into standing still.

"If you really were thieves, she would have called the police, not her private security guards. Now go!"

Ajay and Saif ran through the corridors, ducking and diving and swirling past other lawyers and secretaries and technicians who were tumbling out of their offices to see what was going on.

"Sorry! Excuse me! Sorry again!" Ajay shouted at each person he bumped into. One lawyer with a big mustache spun like a windmill in a hurricane, the papers he was holding letting loose like sails. Saif stopped Ajay from helping the man to pick them up, tugging at him so that they kept running until they reached the elevator—a dark, rusted metal one, nothing like the glass one they had come up in.

"Hurry, Ajay!" begged Saif.

Ajay punched the ground-floor button. He could see Mrs. Pain at the other end of the corridor. Her hair was drenched and plastered to her face, her eyes were wild, and she was running toward them, her hands in front of her as if she wanted to claw them alive.

The elevator doors closed just before she reached them.

Ajay sank to his haunches.

For the moment they were safe.

Chapter Forty

Ajay and Saif were back at the station, telling the story to Vinod and Jai over Indian Chinese noodles that Vinod had made.

"And then," said Saif, in between slurps of noodles, "I put up my fists and said to Mrs. Pain and her thugs, 'You don't frighten me. Leave us alone, or I'll fight you,' and they were so scared they let us get into the elevator."

"What happened after that?" asked Vinod, adding more chili noodles to all their plates.

"The guards on the ground floor tried to catch us, but we ran—fast like the wind!" said Saif.

Ajay nodded, thinking back fondly to the bit where he'd called, "Mouse infestation!" on the way out and hit the alarm, causing all the clients, staff, and lawyers in the reception area to shriek and scream and run around. The guards had been caught up in the mayhem, and by the time they would have gotten themselves free, Ajay and Saif had disappeared into the crowd.

"But aren't you afraid of the police?" said Jai, his eyes piercing. He did not trust the police.

"No," said Ajay. "Mrs. Pain has done something wrong; something illegal. She wouldn't dare to call the police, in case they find out. We're safe." He rubbed his nose. "Now, where's Yasmin? I want to open the file."

"I'm here!" she said, coming in and seating herself on an upturned cardboard box. "What file?"

"This one!" said Saif, pointing to where he had placed it in the center of the table. "It's from the law firm. We were waiting for you before we opened it," he added graciously.

They all turned their heads to the file. It was a red folder. On it was written *The Amanap Papers* in gold print.

"Well, go on then," said Yasmin. "Let's open it."

Ajay coughed, then opened the file. Each of them took out sheets of paper from inside. Ajay had the report from Block Surveyors to Mr. Z's company. He scanned it, his horror growing with every word he read.

"What does the report say, Ajay?" asked Vinod gently.

"To Mr. Z." Ajay's voice was expressionless as he read: *"The factory is not fit for purpose. Structurally the building is weak and is a danger to all those who work inside. The slightest external or internal pressure could cause it to collapse. A particular risk is the weight of water that the monsoons will bring."*

"So Mr. Z knew," whispered Yasmin. "And made us go in there anyway."

"That's not all," said Jai, his golden eyes like a hawk's. "Look at this. It's a diagram showing how the business is organized. Mr. Z owns lots of 'shell' companies that hide his activities. He does all his dirty work through them, but no one realizes that he's the one in control."

"What if there's a problem—like with the factory?" asked Vinod.

Ajay was almost choking in anger, understanding at last. "If there's a problem, the shell company folds. It disappears, and it looks like the whole thing is over. No one can find who is responsible. No one knows that it was owned and completely controlled by Mr. Z."

"So a shell company has nothing to do with shells?" asked Saif, looking a little disappointed.

"No—it's literally just a shell of a company with nothing real underneath, like the FISHY builders," said Ajay.

"But surely people know that these companies are not real—that they're just fake companies owned by Mr. Z?" said Vinod in disbelief.

"It doesn't look like anyone is checking. Look at this—Mr. S.O.S. is listed as a director on loads of these companies, many of them registered in London, and we know that he's a three-year-old! They are putting his name down even without him or his grandmother knowing."

Yasmin's face looked haggard as she turned around the pieces of paper she'd been holding. "Look at this—the land he's planning to build the new slum on, he got cheap because it's contaminated! Mrs. Pain and he have put together a strategy so that no one finds out that he knows. He'll sell the land in a couple of years, before people start going into the hospital with symptoms."

"And this is why he wants to demolish the old slum. He's got an agreement with a multinational company to use the land the old slum is on to build expensive flats on, which he can sell for millions. That's what all this is about . . . greed," said Saif, shaking.

"Ajay, if the new land is poisoned, we need to do something *now*," said Yasmin. "Those excavators start work tomorrow."

"We are going to do something," said Ajay; his voice was very quiet. He stood up and looked at each of them, his mouth set in a sharp line. "Has everyone eaten?"

"Yes, Ajay."

"Is everyone ready?"

"Yes, Ajay!"

"Then, everyone"—he smiled grimly—"we have a paper to run."

Chapter Forty-One

Outside, twilight had fallen in inky blue shadows. They switched on lamps that threw pools of golden light over them as they worked in the engineering rooms. Ajay, his cheeks burning, his eyes fierce, took his mother's pen from behind his ear and wrote as he had never done before: words, sentences, paragraphs poured from his pen, setting out every link in the vicious chain. He was barely conscious of Vinod picking up each sheet of paper as it fell to his side and running to Saif and Jai, who were operating the printing press, setting the type, painting it and pressing it, so page after page of newsprint fell out.

Hours later, although to him it felt like minutes, Ajay scrawled the last words, *Let justice be done though the heavens fall!*, on the final page.

"It's finished?" asked Vinod.

Ajay came back to reality with a sigh of exhaustion and exhilaration. He had never written anything like it before.

"It's done." He jumped down from his chair, put his arm around Vinod, and together they went to the printing press. It was rumbling and whistling, as if it were waiting and eager for the last page of the story.

Saif looked up from where he and Jai were operating the machine.

"This is the last page?" he asked, owl-eyed.

Ajay nodded. Saif took it from him reverently and set the pieces of type. Jai painted the printing plate, and set the printing press to action. Ajay had watched the press at work before, but this felt even more special. Pink page after pink page rolled off the press: his friends' work and his words combined.

They collected the sheets and all went together to Yasmin, who frowned in concentration as she pressed the wooden stamp that she had been carving into ink and then onto each page. Ajay picked up one of the pages, and gasped. Yasmin had always been good at drawing patterns, but the cartoons she had drawn before on the sand were tentative and lacking in confidence. These weren't. Each line was defined, bold and pure, creating the essence of all those involved, and a shadowy figure for Mr. Z, in a few simple strokes. The cartoons had strength, clarity, and power.

"These are wonderful!" said Jai, who had also picked up one of the pages.

Yasmin caught Ajay's eye. "I've been working at it," she said. Then she went back to concentrating on her work.

Remembering their conversation at the beach, Ajay felt his heartbeat quicken.

Finally, all the pages had been gathered and put together. The finished newspapers lay there in piles, ready for them to distribute in a few hours.

"We've done it!" said Saif, almost bouncing with excitement.

"Thanks to you, Saif," said Ajay. "You built the machine and kept it running. You really are the greatest apprentice engineer in Mumbai."

Saif blushed.

Jai was grinning, but then suddenly he frowned. "Did you hear that?"

"Hear what?" said Vinod, taking his proud gaze off the papers for a moment.

Jai looked rattled. "I don't know—it sounded like . . ." He shook his head as if trying to clear his ears. "It sounded like . . ."

There was the sound of doors being opened and booted footsteps coming in.

"Like payback?" said a gravelly voice behind them.

Ajay whirled and saw eight large men standing in the doorway, cracking their knuckles. Mrs. Pain's security guards and members of the gang that had beaten up the old man in the slum and who must be Mr. Z's thugs. One smiled lazily, showing his golden tooth. It gleamed like a bullet in his mouth.

Chapter Forty-Two

Jai reacted first, running toward the men, trying to get to the station alarm that was behind them. One of the men hit him in the stomach. Jai's face creased in pain, but he used both hands to push the thug to the ground with a crash. At that, two other men stepped forward and grabbed Jai's arms, locking them behind him, while a fourth, with a scar across his arm, punched him again, causing Jai's knees to buckle. Jai groaned, almost senseless.

"Let him go!" yelled Ajay. He dived for the man's legs. The man with the scar toppled but another two men took his place. They smashed their knuckled fists into Ajay, causing him to gag and his vision to blur. He tried to raise his arms to protect himself but the blows kept coming, each one like being crushed by a hammer. Next to him, Vinod was crying out under the kicks raining down on him. Ajay could hear Saif howl in terror as he was pinioned to the wall. Yasmin's curses suddenly turned to a shattering scream.

At last, when every bone in his body felt battered and broken, Ajay felt his chin being held up by a man's hand. Ajay pried his eyes open through the bruises. It was the man with the golden tooth—his face so close to Ajay's that he, Ajay, could feel the hot stench of his breath.

"Had enough?" the man said.

Ajay couldn't speak. The others were being held up against the wall: Vinod's nose was bleeding, Jai's lip was ripped open, Yasmin was clutching her arm, which hung at an odd angle at her side, and Saif was cowering next to them, his face bruised purple.

The man with the golden tooth took out a box of matches. *What is he doing?* thought Ajay. And, as if he heard him, the man met his eyes. He took out a match, and slowly struck it against the side of the box. There was a sudden flare of light.

"No!" cried Ajay, suddenly realizing what was about to happen.

The light of the flame reflected in the man's eyes for a moment, twisting and curling.

"You shouldn't have gotten in Mr. Z's way," said the man.

He threw the match. The tiny point of fire landed in the piles of *The Mumbai Sun.*

For a moment, nothing happened. Ajay held his breath. Then the papers seemed to glow from the center. There was a crackle, and the papers disintegrated and collapsed inward into the orange flames that leaped up, darting this way and that, turning the paper white and then black. The flames grew bigger, devouring everything in their path, throwing out waves of heat and smoke.

"Here's the file," said the guard with the scar, his skin looking red in the flames. Ajay saw the folder with *The Amanap Papers* written in gold print on the outside being given to the man with the golden tooth.

"No," he whispered.

The man flicked through it. "This is the file all right. The one Mr. Z said had to be destroyed." He flung it onto the flames, where it lay for a second, then burned to cinders with a scattering of black and gold sparks.

Ajay felt his heart tear in two. His friends were hurt and broken, and the evidence that could have brought justice and stopped the destruction of the slum was gone.

Mr. Z had won.

Chapter Forty-Three

Even destroying *The Mumbai Sun* and the file of evidence wasn't enough for Mr. Z's men.

The thug with the golden tooth put his face close to Ajay's again, so that Ajay could see the strings of spittle in his mouth.

"We're going to make sure that you and your friends never work again," he taunted.

Then he stood up and gave a signal. Three of his men took metal bars that had always stood against the walls and surrounded the printing press. Ajay heard Saif scrambling up in the corner.

Another signal, and the men raised their bars.

Ajay realized at the same time as Saif what they were going to do. He shuddered, wanting to block his ears as he heard Saif beg them: "Please don't hurt it. Please don't hurt it. Please—"

The men brought the bars down, clanging and ringing and reverberating against the press. Metal smashed against metal, throwing out sparks and bits of machinery and springs.

Saif sobbed uncontrollably. Ajay wanted to put his arm around his shoulders and stop him from witnessing what was happening.

Again and again they struck, destroying the machine, crushing it into tiny pieces that scattered and fell, turning red hot in the flames that were steadily growing bigger around them.

Ajay couldn't bear it. It felt as if it was his heart they had broken, not just the printing press.

When they finally stopped and the press had been smashed into smithereens, the men paused to admire their handiwork.

And that was the final straw.

"How could you?" shouted Saif. "How could you destroy it?"

He bit the hand that was holding him against the wall. There was a sudden yelp of pain as the guard who had been holding him jumped up and down in agony. Released, Saif ran to the corner of the room. Ajay didn't understand. What was he doing?

There was no time to think. Using every scrap of energy that he had left, he drove his elbow into the stomach of the man holding him. There was a poof of expelled air as the man bent forward, clutching his belly, letting him go.

Ajay moved to help Yasmin, but there was no need. With her one good hand, she had grabbed hold of a plate lying on the shelf beside her and smashed it into the face of the guard holding her, flattening it like a chapati. She then used the plate as a Frisbee to hit the man holding Jai. The man crumpled.

Jai flashed a lopsided grin to convey his thanks, then turned sharply. Saif was running back from the corner calling his name: "Jai! Catch!"

And suddenly Ajay knew why Saif had run to the corner— it was where Jai kept his cricket bat. Saif threw it. It whirled in the air and Jai caught it, holding it like a sword.

The men with the metal bars turned to him, looking violent and dangerous.

Jai stood ready.

Ajay's brain kicked into gear. Jai couldn't hold them all off with a wooden bat. Ajay clicked his fingers; he had a plan. He looked at Vinod, who understood from the times they had worked together at the station that he had to provide the distraction.

"The fire! The fire!" cried Vinod. "It will burn everything."

Ajay realized that this was not just a statement to distract the men . . . it was true. The heat from the flames was overpowering. Soon they would be uncontrollable. The thugs looked at the raging flames, giving Ajay the chance to run forward, taking out a cricket ball from his pocket.

"Jai—hit this!" he called.

Jai stepped forward.

Ajay bowled.

Jai slammed the ball.

Everyone held their breath.

And then the sound of ringing tore through the station.

Jai had done it! He had hit the alarm.

Chapter Forty-Four

Niresh and the other station attendants began running in.

The thugs dropped their metal bars and scrammed. Ajay wanted to follow them, but the first job was to put out the fire that was now roaring orange and gold and licking at the walls of the room. Some of the attendants had gotten fire extinguishers and were blasting the flames, smothering them with foam. Others were turning on taps to the side, opening up gushes of water. Ajay, Jai, Yasmin, Saif, and Vinod made a chain, passing buckets of water from the taps to the attendants. Water was flung onto patches of fire that went out with sudden gulping hisses and streams of white smoke.

It was dawn before the fire was finally out. Dappling rays of sunlight filtered in through the window.

The exhausted station attendants had gone to make their reports. Niresh had finished helping Yasmin put her arm in a makeshift sling. "The station owes you our thanks for helping to put out the fire," he said, turning to them all.

Ajay felt like weeping. He shook his head. "It was because of me that it started. If I hadn't insisted on writing about Mr. Z . . ."

Yasmin looked up, her eyes stormy. "Stop it, Ajay! This is not your fault!"

Jai raised his face from where he was pressing it with a bag of broken ice cubes. "Yasmin's right. *None* of this is your fault."

"This was work we did together, Ajay," added Saif, who was busy collecting bits of type that had spun out as the printer had been destroyed.

Ajay rubbed his face with his hand. He didn't believe them.

Vinod took a deep breath. "So, what are we going to do now?"

"What can we do? They've won," Ajay said, no expression in his voice. "The excavators are moving into the slum this afternoon, and there's nothing we can do to stop it." He felt the dull echo of the words catch his heart. He wanted to bury his face in his hands and hide away and forget everything that had happened over the last few months.

But that would be cowardly. He owed it to his friends to face them. He took a deep breath and forced himself to look at the others.

He was expecting to see blame or matching helplessness . . .

. . . but all he saw was trust and confidence.

They still believed in him.

He grew angry.

"Aren't you listening?" he said, jumping up. "The papers are destroyed, the evidence is destroyed, even the printer is destroyed." He glared at them. "They've won," he repeated.

"No, they haven't, Ajay bhaiya," said Saif placidly. "You're the editor of *The Mumbai Sun*. You'll think of something."

"But you should hurry," said Vinod. "There's not much time."

Yasmin, Jai, and Niresh looked expectantly at him.

Why didn't they understand that they had lost? Ajay's temper began to fray.

"Uh—excuse me. Can I come in?" said a gentle voice from the door. It was Lata, the junior at Pain and Proffiit Partners, her nut-brown hair sweeping the shoulders of her jacket.

"Sit down," said Jai courteously, making room on the bench for her as she came in. She sat down, looking uncomfortable, as if unsure of her welcome.

"Who are you?" asked Vinod, clearly confused.

"I worked with Mrs. Pain," said Lata.

"She fired you?" asked Saif, in shock.

"I resigned." She looked at them and gave a small smile. "I should have done it ages ago actually. I knew Mrs. Pain was a bully, but I didn't know she was corrupt until yesterday."

"What about your sick mother?" asked Ajay.

Lata smiled gently. "Mom's the one who told me to resign."

"Why are you here?" said Vinod.

Lata took a file out of her bag. "I have a contribution to make to your news story. It's a copy of the Amanap file you had, but with additional handwritten notes from Mrs. Pain. The file sets out the names and criminal activities of everyone involved— from surveyors to members of the police." Amusement flickered in her face. "It's photocopied, and straight to the exact milli-meter. The only thing missing is the surveyor's report."

"But where did you get it?" asked Ajay, taking the file from her and flicking through it. He saw a copy of a memo from Mrs. Pain and an official-looking document stuck on the final page. It hadn't been in the file they had stolen from the safe.

"No honor among thieves. Mrs. Pain kept it at her home, so that she could use it to blackmail everyone else if she ever needed to. She wanted me to make a copy in case the client sent his goons to rob her place."

"I don't understand," said Saif. "Why get you involved?"

"She knew I was desperate. But everyone has a line that they won't cross—or, at least, they should." Lata's eyes danced. "I've always been terrified of Mrs. Pain. That stopped when I saw her screaming at you with the bucket on her head."

Ajay stood up, his body tingling. He felt his confidence, and his anger, return. The memo was the last piece of the puzzle. He understood it all now. *The Mumbai Sun* had evidence and it had good people on its side. As editor, he had to make sure that no one stopped the truth from coming out. What had the old woman asked of him? Be smart and honest. Ajay grinned.

"He's got a plan," said Saif comfortably to the others.

Chapter Forty-Five

The sun was high in the sky, its light shining down in heavy golden bars onto the slum, glazing everything in its syrupy light.

Ajay reached the far edge of the slum. A huge crowd had gathered there, holding what possessions they could, looking wary and watchful. Ajay pushed his way through. This time he was not going to go up the tree to ask questions. He was going to be at the front with the other journalists.

A line of pink ribbon was all that separated the slum from the excavators on the other side. Towering above them all, blocking the light, the excavators looked like monsters eager to eat—their serrated blades hovering just above the ground. Ajay squared his shoulders.

Mrs. Shania was holding the mic, her sapphire earrings catching the light like chips of blue ice. Standing next to her was Mr. Raz, in a gleaming white suit, and then Mrs. Pain.

Mrs. Shania began to speak. "And so, we have finally arrived at this wonderful moment for our city. The moment where we say 'no' to unhygienic places and poverty, where we say 'no more' to disease and filth, where we say 'never again' to—"

"Excuse me," interrupted Mr. Gupta, the editor of *The City Paper*. "But why haven't the residents of the slum been moved to their new homes before the excavators start work?"

"That is a very good question," said Mrs. Shania, smiling at him. Mr. Gupta did not smile back. The expression on his face was grim. She continued quickly, "It is just taking a little longer than expected. Rest assured, all is in hand." And before Mr. Gupta could ask another question, she turned. "And now I hand over to Mr. Raz: one of the most respected, caring, and philanthropic men in Mumbai. An environmentalist who is feted throughout the world. We are lucky to have him here, endorsing this project that will change the face of our beloved city forever."

She handed Mr. Raz a pair of silver scissors to cut the ribbon. He took them with a smile on his face.

The smile suddenly froze as Ajay stepped forward.

"Mr. Raz doesn't deserve respect," said Ajay, his voice loud and clear, the words on the memo attached to Lata's file emblazoned in his mind. "He is a crook, a blackmailer, and a murderer. He needs to be stopped."

Chapter Forty-Six

The silence that followed Ajay's statement had the weight of an elephant.

It was only broken by Mrs. Shania dropping her mic.

The sound brought Mrs. Pain to life. "What are you doing alive?" she hissed, going rigid where she was standing next to Mr. Raz. Her expression twisted as if she had just eaten a lemon . . . whole. "Our men were meant to have . . ."

She blinked, suddenly realizing that they were not alone and that everyone was watching.

Ajay moved closer. "Meant to have what? Destroyed the papers? Meant to have destroyed the evidence showing that you and Mr. Raz"—his voice ignited with fury as he thought back to the revelation in the memo—"or should I use his real name, Mr. Z?—are corrupt and blackmailers?" His temper exploded. "Meant to have hurt my friends?"

"Don't forget the printer!" piped up Saif, appearing next to him.

Ajay nodded. "Meant to have destroyed the printing press of *The Mumbai Sun*? Meant to have started the fire in the railway station? In *my home*?"

Every member of the crowd knew how dangerous a fire could be. The air changed, becoming electric with hostility.

Mr. Raz looked around and laughed, but there was a false

note to it. "This boy is talking nonsense. I am an environmentalist. I have done nothing but good. Look at the people who hang on my every word—not just here, but across the world."

Despite all his crimes, and everything he has done to hide his identity, Mr. Raz still considers himself a good person? thought Ajay in disbelief.

"They haven't investigated far enough to find the truth. You are no environmentalist. The papers show that instead of planting trees you have been cutting them down. The truth is that you're nothing but a corrupt, murderous hypocrite," Ajay blazed.

Mr. Raz turned to him. "You have no proof that those men were anything to do with me."

"Except for Mrs. Pain's own words just a few moments ago that suggest that you both do know something about this," said Mr. Gupta quietly, his eyes focused on Ajay. "My reporters also spoke of signs of a fire from the railway station this morning."

"This is ridiculous!" said Mr. Raz.

"Is it?" said Ajay. He picked up the mic that Mrs. Shania had dropped, turned to face the crowd, and took out pages of faluda-pink paper. "I am the editor of *The Mumbai Sun*. Many of you know our newspaper already. We have been investigating the collapse of the factory that cost Mr. Gir his life. What we found was a road—a motorway—of dirty dealings, that led straight to Mr. Raz."

"This is an outrageous accusation!" said Mrs. Shania. "Police!" she shrieked. "Arrest that boy immediately for disrupting the peace!"

"Let him finish," said Mr. Gupta calmly. "The public will be the judge here, not you. And if the police step one inch over the line, I will personally make sure that every broadcaster in India knows about it."

Mr. Raz went pale.

Chapter Forty-Seven

Ajay nodded to Mr. Gupta for warning off the police. "Thank you. Now, Mr. Raz and Mrs. Pain got their thugs to set fire to our papers, but they didn't count on our apprentice engineer, Saif, creating a handheld roller from the type. We now have twenty-one copies of the newspaper." There was a cheering from the crowd. Saif waved. "My friends—many of whom you already know—Niresh, Jai, Vinod, and Yasmin"—each stepped forward from the crowd when their name was called and waved to cheers and clapping—"will distribute twenty of these copies. If you have a mobile phone, take pictures and send them on."

Jai started distributing to the journalists, who were already taking out their phones.

Vinod started distributing to the people from the slum.

Yasmin started distributing to the factory workers.

Niresh started distributing to all the people who knew him from traveling on the railways.

Saif went behind the stage.

"If you don't have a mobile phone, or can't see a copy," Ajay continued, "listen to me as I read the article they didn't want you to see."

"Stop this farce now!" said Mr. Raz to Mrs. Shania.

"And how exactly do you propose I do that?" said Mrs. Shania bitingly. "This is your mess. It is not mine."

Ajay ignored them and slowly started to read the article: He told the crowd how Mr. Raz was not an environmentalist at all, but actually the Bollygarch Mr. Z who used shell companies to hide his ownership of them; how the factory was deliberately built cheaply and dangerously; how Mr. Raz had hidden the surveyor's report and then bribed the surveyors to keep it hidden. Mr. Gir's widow started to cry silently as she heard the catalogue of crimes.

At one point, Mrs. Pain tried to slip away to the left, but Yasmin and members of the factory who had known Mr. Gir blocked her path. The dangerous look in Yasmin's eyes meant it was Mrs. Pain who backed away. At another point, Mr. Raz tried to slip away to the right. He was stopped by Jai and the cricket team, who stood in front of him silent and impassable. For the first time in his life, Mr. Raz began to look afraid.

Ajay wrapped up by telling the crowd how Mr. Raz was going to make a profit from the land the slum was standing on, and how the land earmarked for the residents was contaminated.

When he finished, the crowd was no longer just hostile—or even angry—it was incandescent with rage. It was the rage of people who have been bullied by the rich and the powerful their whole lives; of people seen as expendable statistics rather than human; of people who have suffered the consequences of the arrogance and ruthlessness of those in power. The crowd's rage was like a furnace. If unleashed, it would obliterate everything in its path. Everyone stepped forward, their fists clenched.

"You have no proof," said Mr. Raz, but his voice was weak, and he was trembling. He could feel the wrath of the crowd too.

"None at all," said Mrs. Pain, grabbing on to this possible lifeline, not daring to look at the children she would happily have allowed to become sick on contaminated ground.

"Actually, he does," said a man with wistful eyes, pushing his way to the front. Ajay recognized him as the pale-faced surveyor that he'd gone to see with Yasmin and who he had called a coward. The man was no longer pale though; the color was high in his cheeks.

"I am the surveyor who made a report on the factory, stating that it was unsafe. Our firm accepted bribes to keep quiet about our findings."

Ajay felt a quiver of fear as the crowd directed its anger toward the man.

"Stop," Ajay said to him. "You don't need to do this now."

The surveyor shook his head. "I need to confront what I have done. I did not know about the bribe until you came to our firm, but I kept silent anyway because I was afraid. If I had spoken out, Mr. Gir might still be alive. It's too late to help him, but maybe by doing this I'll help others."

Ajay bowed his head. Jai had been right. People were worth more than the worst thing they had done.

"That man's word means nothing!" cried out Mrs. Pain. "He's lying."

The crowd became very still. The atmosphere was, thought Ajay, like a pressure cooker about to boil over in all directions.

"No, he's not, but you are," said Lata, stepping daintily out from the crowd. "I worked with Mrs. Pain," she said, speaking to them directly. "I can confirm that there is written proof of everything that Ajay has said, all set out in a file called the Amanap Papers. In Mrs. Pain's private copy, that she kept for her own protection, are also a memo and official documentation that set out that Mr. Raz is none other than Mr. Z. I have sent a copy of that file to the bar council and the police."

"They won't—"

"Do anything?" Lata smiled. "Have you seen what's happening here? Do you really think that anyone is going to protect you after this?"

"You'll never work as a lawyer again. You'll be known as a whistleblower—someone who is not loyal to her employer."

Lata shrugged. "If the employer is doing something wrong, and being a whistleblower stops them, I can't think of anything I'd be prouder to call myself."

Mr. Raz looked at them all with desperation. "You don't understand. This was all for the good of India. What good are plantings of trees unless you turn them into building materials? My wealth has created jobs, allowed money to trickle down, increased our GDP . . ." His voice trailed off. Ajay met his eyes. *It must be strange to believe you are cleverer, more manipulative, and better than anyone else your whole life, and suddenly to be found out as just another hypocrite and parasite, living off the work of others to benefit yourself.*

Mr. Raz's desperation turned to a tantrum. "This is not going to be the end of this!"

What's he going to do? thought Ajay suddenly. He looked capable of anything.

"You think that you people can stop me?" Mr. Raz shouted, out of control, waving the scissors in his hand. Ajay felt a stab of fear. "I have the contract to destroy this slum, and that is what is going to happen!" He took the scissors in his hand and moved to the ribbon.

"No!" shouted Ajay.

The ribbon fell apart.

Ajay felt a wave of terror.

At the signal, seen by the drivers, the excavators' red lights came on. The ignitions were turned. People screamed in panic, trying to get away. The blades came up, the sunlight glinting off their sharp edges, ready to plunge into the ground below.

Ajay had miscalculated. Despite everything, the slum would be destroyed and people would die.

He stepped forward, holding up his hand, as if somehow by that small action he could protect all the people behind him.

The blades started to come down.

Ajay squeezed his eyes shut.

And the blades froze in midair.

The engines snapped off.

Ajay opened his eyes and looked up. Saif was seated on top of one of the excavators, waving and holding fragments of machinery in his hand. He'd done it. He'd dismantled the excavators as planned.

Just in time.

Ajay waved back and drew a long, long breath of relief.

Chapter Forty-Eight

Ajay smiled. The sun was shining, the grass was green, and the smell of frying samosas was in the air. The story of *The Mumbai Sun* had been picked up by every national paper in India. Mr. Raz, Mrs. Pain, and the thugs, including the man with the golden tooth, had all been arrested; Lata and the surveyor had found different jobs; there had been a crackdown on shell companies across India . . . and Mr. Gupta had offered Ajay a position on *The City Paper.*

"You and your team got to the truth of a story that we should have," Mr. Gupta had said to him, coming to the railway station that morning. Dawn had turned the platform a dusky shade of peach. "Not only that, you've got people reading newspapers again. You've shown that we still have a role." He had pointed to the commuters. Many were reading papers. Even those on their phones showed screens that were bright pink with the copies of *The Mumbai Sun* that had been photographed.

Ajay had shrugged, embarrassed and delighted all at once.

"Thanks to you, people have seen the value of facts, and news that goes beyond clickable headlines. My paper is selling again. Once you're fourteen, you've got a job on the paper if you want it. Not any job either; a job as a reporter. We could do with your observation skills, your tenacity, and your courage."

"Thank you!" Ajay had said in amazement. "But . . ." Why

was he hesitating? It was everything he had ever wanted, every dream that he'd ever had come true . . . he should be jumping up and down, saying yes, shaking Mr. Gupta's hand. So why wasn't he?

Mr. Gupta had clocked the pause. "Look—think about it. Tell me by the end of the day."

Ajay had nodded.

And now he was daydreaming—thinking of the job offer and the sunshine and the samosas—when a cricket ball landed in front of him, creating a haze of dust.

"Ajay! Wake up! Come on, we've got to help the others," said Yasmin.

Ajay broke out of his reverie and looked around. They were in the outdoor cricket stadium of the private school. The sun was shining off the seats, the smell of fresh paint and polish was in the air and the grass was bright green. People were milling around before the start of the match—families of boys, dignitaries, businesspeople, journalists. News of the contest between the slum kids and the best junior cricket team in India had spread like wildfire. It wasn't just the rich and powerful who were there—it felt as if half of the slum had gathered to support Jai and the rest of the team by holding up and waving colorfully painted cardboard signs.

"Hey, Vinod!"

Vinod was busy in his chef's cap and uniform, manning outdoor stations with a huge sign written and decorated by Yasmin on a bolt of cloth reading POP-UP RESTAURANT OF THE SECRET COOK OF THE MUMBAI SUN!!! People were jostling each other in the queue; coming back for second, third, and even fourth helpings.

"Let me help!" said Ajay.

"You're sure you're here to help and not to eat?" said Vinod, his eyebrow raised.

Ajay felt a pained expression cross his face at being accused of such a terrible crime.

"As if I, the editor of *The Mumbai Sun*, would do such a thing!"

Vinod grinned and pointed to the kulfi stand, where Saif was serving the rich ice creams—helping himself to one scoop out of every ten; his bowl full of lemon, rose, and pistachio ices that were melting together in a glistening sugary rainbow.

"Being an apprentice engineer is hungry work!" Saif said defiantly when he saw them looking in his direction. He held his bowl behind him protectively.

"It's okay, Saif, the Headmaster said that we can eat as much as we want—but leave room for the rest of dessert!" said Vinod.

Saif nodded vigorously.

As Ajay served the food, his stomach rumbled. Earlier, the Headmaster had provided the school's kitchen facilities and the budget for the ingredients when Ajay had suggested that Vinod do the catering for the cricket match. Vinod had almost fallen to the ground at the sum.

"Are . . . are you sure?" he had asked.

The Headmaster had nodded, his expression serene. "I've been hearing a lot about the 'Secret Cook of the Mumbai Sun.'

Just provide the best banquet you can. I am sure that it will be worth it. It will be a good way to celebrate the cricket match and, after all these years, the renaming of the school to the Satyameva Jayate School."

With nothing to stop him from making the dishes of his imagination into reality, Vinod had surpassed himself. There were buttered rice dishes fragrant with cardamom and cloves, soft and chewy naan breads with fillings of juicy raisins and sweet coconut, curries of stewed squash and lime leaves, lacy dosa pancakes stuffed with potatoes, and sugared sweetmeats of ground almonds, with silver paste, cut into diamonds. Ajay could see people around him lick their lips as they scraped their dishes clean.

A sudden tussle broke his attention. He looked up from where he was serving and saw a man pushing through others in the line. Mahesh! He felt his blood boil at the thought of this man who, as owner of the restaurant, had so often left Vinod bruised and frightened. He took his place at Vinod's side.

But Vinod was no longer frightened. He waited patiently as Mahesh reached him.

"Why, you . . ." Mahesh swore.

"Yes?" said Vinod calmly.

"You work for me!"

"Actually," said Vinod, wiping the surface in front of him down with a cloth. "I don't. You sacked me from the restaurant. Remember?"

A slender woman dressed in a canary-yellow sari and topaz earrings looked up from where she was polishing off her second helping. "You sacked him?" she asked Mahesh, and shook her head slowly. "Big mistake."

Mahesh took a deep breath. "You may not realize it, but this boy is an untouchable."

The woman laughed, looking like a ray of sunshine in the light. "Firstly, I feel sorry for you for still thinking in those terms. Secondly, discrimination against people for untouchability is against the constitution *and has been for over sixty years*, so you're not just wrong, you're hopelessly out of date. Thirdly, a chef this good could be from Mars for all I care." She turned to Vinod and gave him an embellished card. "Contact me when this is all over. I may have an opportunity that will interest you." She turned back to Mahesh with appraising eyes. "You've shown yourself to be prejudiced and a fool. Once word gets out about that, your restaurant business is likely to be over. Be nice to this chef, if for no other reason than the fact that you might be begging him for a job in a few years. Now, if you'll excuse me, I'm going to treat myself to a third helping. It's not every day I get to eat food this good!" She winked at the boys and left.

Vinod took a look at her card and, seeing her name, gasped as if he'd just been told he could go on an all-expenses trip to the moon. Ajay already knew who she was—The Canary, the most important food critic in Mumbai, whose word could make, or break, a restaurant—after all, he was the one who had invited her.

Mahesh, meanwhile, was sweating with fear and anger that he could not unleash in public. Feeling that he should be gracious in Mahesh's time of defeat, Ajay gave him a bowl of watermelon-pink kulfi. Its sweetness could not save Mahesh's restaurant, but perhaps it would help him to cool off.

That the ice cream happened to be the same color as *The Mumbai Sun* was just a happy coincidence and, like Mahesh's invitation to the cricket match by Ajay, not preplanned at all.

Chapter Forty-Nine

It was almost time for the cricket match to start. They were all sitting in their seats around the blazing green of the cricket ground, waiting expectantly. Ajay craned his neck and waved as he saw Mr. S.O.S. and then Mr. S.O.S.'s grandmother, who had been turned out of the custard-yellow house and were now living in a shared shelter in the slum, and farther along in the same row of seats, Lata and her mother (who was now out of the hospital), the surveyor, Niresh, and Mr. Gupta.

"It should be a good game," said the Headmaster, rubbing his hands expectantly.

Ajay nodded happily—his chin in his hands, his elbows on his knees—ready to relax and enjoy this cricket match that he had fought so hard to bring about.

"Ajay!"

Ajay looked up to see Jai, dressed in cricket whites, running up to them, his dark hair almost copper in the sunlight and his eyes full of panic.

"You're going to have to join the team, Ajay! We're one short. Our star bowler—he twisted his ankle on the way here."

Ajay blinked, "But, Jai. I am the editor of *The Mumbai Sun*." Then he added, with emphasis, "I am *not* a cricketer," in case Jai had mistakenly confused the two.

"You know how to play cricket and you can bowl. I've seen you. That's all we need, now come on!"

Saif, on his other side, pushed him forward. "Do your best, Ajay. And remember that it is very easy to bowl; you just need to think like an apprentice engineer—about geometry and acceleration."

"Geometry and acceleration?" said Jai.

"And that sort of thing," added Saif vaguely, with the air of a king who should not be made to explain trifling matters.

Ten minutes later, Ajay was dressed in cricket whites borrowed from the school, and still repeating the words *geometry and acceleration* under his breath like a prayer. Watching a cricket match was one of the most tranquil ways to spend a weekend afternoon—however, playing in one, Ajay realized, was very different. His knees were shaking.

The school's cricket team came out. Ajay felt a twinge of fear. They were not known as some of the best junior cricketeers in Mumbai for nothing. They looked sleek, well fed, and powerful.

Ajay saw Bharat, captain of the school cricket team and the boy who had spat at Jai in the street, crossing the pitch and standing opposite Jai. Bharat won the toss, and the look he gave to the crowd, his eyes finally settling on Ajay, was full of triumph and contempt. Ajay could read his thoughts as if he were shouting them out loud: *Last time I was on your home turf. This time you're on mine!*

Ajay took his place on the field. It was a Twenty20 match, so twenty overs, with each over being made up of six balls. Bharat's team had chosen to bat first. The opening batsman stood ready, the arrogance on his face clear to everyone on the pitch. The bowler, who Ajay recognized as one of Jai's friends with a nose that had been broken in a fight somewhere, looked as nervous as Ajay felt. It was as if, like Ajay, he too felt like an impostor on these sunlit grounds. Jai's friend was normally a great spin bowler, but his first ball went wide and his second was hit for a four. The batsman looked at him lazily. "Is this really the best that you can do?"

Jai's friend didn't answer. For another four balls it seemed that it was. All four balls were hit superbly well, leading to a sigh of disappointment from the crowd. Ajay bit his lip. The team from the slum seemed hopelessly outmatched.

And then, halfway into the third over, the batsman hit a ball that flew sharply in the air. Ajay's heart sank into his boots, because it looked like this one would be a six. But Jai jumped up, seeming to leap into the air out of nowhere, and caught the ball.

For a moment there was silence. Then the crowd erupted into cheers. Supporters of the team from the slum took up a chant, leading to startled looks from the parents around them: "Jai! Jai! Jai!"

Jai's catch brought confidence back into the team. The bowler made some balls turn sharply and two other batsmen were out one after another. The next batter was able to make only a couple of runs before he too was out with a keen bit of fielding from the team. Ajay felt hope skip a beat inside him. The bowling was changed twice but the school team steadily built up runs.

The last bowler they tried was lightning fast but erratic.

The batsman he faced was tall and flexed his muscles. *No doubt piled on at the school gym*, thought Ajay sourly. He hit well. He and his partner worked as a team and quickly hit several runs. At each run, Ajay felt more and more uncertain of whether the team from the slum would ever be able to catch up when it was their turn to bat.

The bowler bowled another fast ball. The batsman hit it. It flew into the air, and then, like a diving bird, curved sharply down toward Ajay. Finally, a chance to fight back! The crowd gasped, clutching on to one another, equal parts hope and horror. Ajay felt time slowing down as the speck in the air became larger and larger as it hurtled toward him. He raised his hands, ready to pluck it from the air. Ajay felt it touch his fingertips. He thought he'd gotten it!

But he had miscalculated. It slipped off his fingertips and rolled over the boundary.

A four.

Ajay lifted his head. The whole crowd was looking at him, half in their seats, their mouths open, a mixture of shock and scorn. His eyes squeezed shut; the beautiful sunshine became clouded. He had failed them all. Most of all, he had failed Jai. The team would have been better off without him.

And then, with the worst possible timing, he heard the captain call his name. It was his turn to bowl.

Chapter Fifty

He walked slowly up to the wicket, feeling Jai's friends' eyes on him. By letting Jai down, he'd let them down too.

The batsman waited. Ajay could hear whispers in the crowd. He tried to pull his thoughts together and concentrate, but it felt as if all of his energy had seeped out when the ball had fallen out of his hands. The first ball was a no-ball.

He tried again. The batsman hit it high with ease. It was just unfortunate for the batsman and the school team that Jai's friend with the broken nose was waiting for the ball, and, unlike Ajay, did not drop it. The crowd clapped, and the batsman left the pitch.

Perhaps there is still a chance, thought Ajay.

Then he saw who was coming onto the pitch and his fear returned.

Bharat stood in front of him as if he owned the pitch, which, in a way, he did. His grin was wolfish. Two balls hit for fours. A weight of depression fell over the crowd. The defeat of the team from the slum felt inevitable. Ajay felt his arms trembling.

And then Bharat made a mistake.

"What did you think you were doing, daring to play against my team? Why don't you all go back to the slum where you belong?" he whispered, so that only Ajay could hear.

Ajay's eyes narrowed, anger turning to energy that coursed

184

through his veins. If he was no more than anyone else here, he was no less either. He ran, twisting his wrist at the last moment. Bharat hit the spinning ball, but only just, shock lining his face. Ajay ran again, and again, each ball spinning faster than the last.

And finally, with a loud thwack, Ajay knocked the bails off the stumps. His team cheered.

Bharat was out!

The score to beat at the end of the twenty overs was 180.

Chapter Fifty-One

The team gathered together in the interval.

"There's no way that we can win!" said Jai's friend with the broken nose.

"Agreed," said the fast bowler. "They've got too many for us."

Jai, his arms crossed, his head down, was very quiet.

Ajay felt a moment of fear that Jai had given up, but then he lifted his head and smiled, the sweep of his golden eyes taking them all in.

"Who here thought we'd even get to this point?" Jai asked softly.

The rest of the team shook their heads.

"Exactly. None of us. But we fought to be here, just like we're going to fight to win this game."

His confidence settled on them all. The signal came for the match to restart. It was their turn to bat . . . and they were going to enjoy every minute of it.

The opening batsmen went in and played well. But the fielding by the school was good . . . really good. The school team ran hard, dived to stop the ball, and threw in quickly. The batsmen were getting runs in singles, but nothing more than that. Soon, several wickets had fallen and it was Jai's turn to bat.

As Jai stepped onto the pitch, the crowd hushed. There was

a sense of electricity around him. Jai took his place, his gold eyes glinting in the sun. The bowler spun as hard as he could, but Jai hit it. It flew over the boundary. A six!

"Yes! Jai!" shouted Ajay.

He wasn't the only one. Even parents of the students looked excited. As much as they loved their kids, they loved a good show of cricket more. It was part of being Indian. Ajay had heard of weddings being postponed in Mumbai because a test match had gone on longer than expected. As the bowler readied for a second ball, Ajay heard the crowd, as one, draw a breath. Was Jai's first bat a chance piece of luck? With a fluid elegance, Jai hit the second ball. Another six.

"Go, Jai!" cried the other teammates.

Ajay saw Yasmin, Saif, and Vinod doing a little dance in the crowd.

He relaxed as Jai hit a four, another six, a four . . .

. . . and kept going as another bowler replaced the second, and the third . . .

. . . and before long, Jai reached a century.

At that, even the Headmaster shot up from his seat and cheered. Ajay wondered for a moment if the Headmaster would get in trouble for being disloyal to the school team, but realized that the entire crowd was standing and cheering with whoops, stamping of feet, and shouts. They knew a cricket star when they saw one. Even the school's cricket team paused for a moment to acknowledge Jai's command of the game, hitting him across the shoulders and clapping. Ajay held back as Jai was hugged by his teammates, but Jai's eyes met his, lit from within, and he mouthed, "Thank you!" Ajay smiled widely and shook his head.

Only one thing spoiled Ajay's joy in that moment—Bharat coming to take his position to bowl. Unlike his teammates, he wore an expression of disgust. When the crowd finally grew quiet again, he ran, and each movement was edged in tense anger. Three overs, tightly controlled. Jai still scored runs, but fewer. There were no theatrics now. Jai was focused on winning the game.

So was Bharat. The ball practically hissed as it left his hand each time. Four balls left. Perhaps it was his anger that made the ball come out of nowhere and smack fast against the bat. Two runs.

Jai's friend was now on strike. Another fast ball, and Jai's friend was out—LBW.

"You're in, Ajay!" came the shout from the batting line.

Ajay looked around. Who were they talking to?

"Ajay—yours!" Jai's friend with the broken nose said. "Get up there."

"But I can't bat," stammered Ajay. "I'm a—"

"Yes, we know, you are the editor of *The Mumbai Sun*."

"I was going to say bowler," said Ajay with as much dignity as he could muster.

"Well, you're our last man. And it's just our luck that it's up to you to win the match. You just need to hold steady and make two runs. It's the last ball."

Ajay gulped as he took his position.

Jai gave him a quick salute, as if to say, *Don't worry.*

Easy for him. Jai was tall and liked it when a ball was coming toward him faster than a steam train. Ajay did not. Ajay liked watching cricket, and occasionally bowling. He did not like feeling like a pin in a bowling alley.

Bharat was throwing the cricket ball up and down, like an upside-down yo-yo. "I'm looking forward to collecting on our bet," he said. "I'm going to bring you to your knees." Then he ran and bowled. Ajay felt his eyes shut automatically at the sight of the ball whizzing toward him.

It went past him, and he heard the umpire call "wide." Now just one more run to get.

Ajay opened his eyes in relief, and shame.

"A practice, Ajay," said Bharat. "This last ball is going to hurt."

Ajay's heart beat slowly. He could see Yasmin, Saif, and Vinod all clutching one another, excitement and trust in their eyes, and Jai, his stance full of quiet confidence. He thought back to the saving of the slum, the justice they had gotten for Mr. Gir, the success of *The Mumbai Sun* and everything else that had happened in the last few months. He turned back to Bharat, his eyes open.

Bharat bowled.

Ajay swung the bat.

He had hit the ball! But only just . . .

"Run!" cried Jai.

Ajay ran. He just needed to make it to the stumps at the other end. In the corner of his eye he could see the crowd surging to their feet, hear the screaming, feel the ball being thrown toward the stumps. He reached out with his bat and slid it over the crease.

It was just a fraction of a second before the ball hit the stumps, but it was enough. Ajay dropped the bat and promptly collapsed on the ground.

He and Jai had done it.

The team from the slum had won.

Chapter Fifty-Two

Ajay and Jai were carried on the shoulders of their teammates to the podium. The Headmaster could hardly keep from grinning as he presented Jai with a gold trophy and Ajay and the rest of the team with gold medals. Bharat was there too. "Under the terms of the bet that I lost, I now—" he began.

"It was a good match, Bharat bhai," said Ajay, stopping him from saying anything more.

Jai held out his hand. "We are grateful to have had the chance to play against your team."

Bharat looked at them in disbelief. His expression was still sour, but there was the tiniest glint of humor underneath. "So grateful you would consider another match next year?"

Jai nodded. And the boys shook hands.

The crowd erupted. As Ajay took out his mother's pen and the spiral notebook to take notes, people in the slum, used to being ignored or insulted, were clasping hands and sharing tears of joy with the people sitting next to them: members of Mumbai society, rich enough to be helicoptered in to see the match.

"We're seeing history being made, my friend," said Mr. Gupta, standing next to Ajay. "It's why we do this job, after all—to see, to observe, and to write it all down."

"Mr. Gupta, about your offer . . ."

"You're not taking it," said Mr. Gupta.

"It's not that I wouldn't be proud to work at your newspaper," Ajay said slowly. "It's just that I belong to *The Mumbai Sun*."

Mr. Gupta sighed, then put his hand on Ajay's shoulder. "I understand. Perhaps it's better that way. Your newspaper serves the city by getting stories that others can't. It would be a shame if it stopped." He turned to go.

"Mr. Gupta?"

"Yes, Ajay?"

"I'll see you at the next story."

Mr. Gupta's face broke into a craggy smile. "You can count on it, Ajay."

Vinod, Yasmin, Saif, and Jai were walking toward him as Ajay finished scribbling down his notes.

"What was that about, Ajay?" asked Vinod.

Ajay took a deep breath. "He offered me a position on the paper."

"Did you accept?" asked Yasmin, her voice low.

Ajay shook his head. "No, I told him the truth—that I belong to *The Mumbai Sun*."

"That is very good," said Saif, sniffing. "I am sure that *The City Paper* has very good people on their staff, but they do not have an apprentice engineer!"

"Or a crusading cartoonist," said Yasmin.

"Or a champion sports editor," said Jai.

"Or a not-so-secret food writer," said Vinod.

Ajay looked at them, blinked back the sudden moisture in his eyes, and smiled. He put his spiral notebook back in his pocket and his mother's pen behind his ear.

"We should go back home," he said. Then, trying to cover up the emotion that he felt, he said, "After all, we have a paper to write."

"And leftovers to eat," said Saif, nodding.

Together, arm in arm, he, Vinod, Saif, Yasmin, and Jai walked back to the railway station, ready to produce the next, very special, sports edition of their newspaper: *The Mumbai Sun*.

Acknowledgments

To Lou Kuenzler and the former and current City Lit workshop and class members who have taught, helped, and encouraged me throughout, and have become some of my closest friends—thank you for everything. The reality is that this book could only have been written with you there.

For encouraging me to write this book: Sheila, Mike, Alice, Louise, David, Hugo, Zoë, Gavin, Oscar, Tilly, Nick, Katie, Stacy, Freddie, Archie, Isla, Euri, Oskar, Leo, Yoko, Chris, Hiroto, Yukina, Tomoko San, Sunagawa San and family, Joanne, Jock, Samantha, Alistair, Peter, Wendy and family, Vince, Anthony, Jen, Jon, Pru, Cynthia, Matt, Nathan, Florence, Rhonda, Kevin, Rebecca, Victoria, Reena, Will, Tara, John, Sarah, Eva, Nahid, Chris, Bob, Savannah, LSF, Julie and family, Andrew, Alexandra and Alex and family, Tosin, Toyin and family, Charlie, Melissa and family, Shelly, Lenka, Rajay, Sujay, Matt, Hayley, Christopher, Megan, Jonathan, Alexander, Ashok, Kayoko, Robert, Hisako, Yoshioka San, Naoto, Mayu, Ken, Belinda, Won-Joo, Geoff, "the Wombats," and the basketball and cricket players.

To my mum, dad, and sister, Puja, and to my cousins, and Rasik, Manjula, Kanchan, and Keshu.

To my wonderful friends, and to my teachers at school and university. To Joanna B and everyone I met through the Faber Academy, especially Nick (for the two thousand words!), Chopra & Chai, O&C, Mrs. Woods, Kieran, Arvon tutors, Tobias H, Clare P,

Dan B, and Elly B. To the current and former staff and students of the Centre D'éducation Des Adultes Amqui, and friends and neighbors in Kurayoshi and Quebec.

To Barry Cunningham and everyone at Chicken House for championing this book and making a dream come true. To Elizabeth Haylett Clark. In memory of Vera, Nancy Silver, Sir Derek, Tejal, and Sandy Millar.

And finally to all the students I have taught—wherever you are, I wish you joy.

About the Author

Varsha Shah loves books that blend humor and story and has always wanted to be a writer. She has had nonfiction articles published in *Legal Week, economia, Harper's Bazaar,* and the *Times Education Supplement.* A former Solicitor, she is now an English Language and Literature teacher. She has also taught English as a foreign language in Japan and Canada, and often draws on her travels in her writing.